Accidental

TRYST

Mia London

Publisher: Mia London Books
PO Box 93852
Southlake, TX 76092

Cover photo by DepositPhoto.
Cover design by Star Crossed Covers.

DEDICATION

To every married couple.

Marriage isn't always easy. But cheers to you all who recognize that you might have something good enough to fight for.

Special thanks to my husband. I know I'm not always the easiest person to live with. I'm thankful for your love, patience, and support. Twenty-one years together and still counting. Eternally yours!

CHAPTER ONE

A ngie's stomach churned at the sloppy wet spot left on her neck. They rolled over, and she reached beneath her to pull a stubborn pillow from under her butt. She threw it to the floor of their bedroom. Mac kept pumping while he leaned down to kiss her shoulder, sucking her skin. More wetness. Angie fought the urge to wipe it off, along with the urge to grimace.

How much longer?

She clasped his shoulders, which were still well-defined and toned after all these years. Of course, Mac worked out diligently at the gym. He trained hard to keep in shape. Despite all that, he didn't turn her on like he once had. Definitely not like when they'd first started dating.

Back then, they'd had sex all the time. She remembered one epic session where they'd completely lost track of time. Mac's roommate had strolled in from the bars at four in the morning, and they'd just looked at each other and snickered. Sleep hadn't mattered.

They'd lived on coffee and lust.

Back then, he'd wake her up, and kiss and stroke her body until she panted with desire before sliding his divine cock inside her. Multiple orgasms were so common she had to force Mac to take a break before she went into a sexual coma.

Now, she needed lubricant and rarely orgasmed. Sex wasn't high on her priority list, her to-do list, or any other kind of list. She'd rather read a book, soak in the tub, or go grocery shopping.

Shit! That reminded her. The boys needed more sliced meat for their lunches.

Crap! How much longer?

Mac froze in mid-pump. "What?"

Her eyes flew open. "What?"

"Did you just say, 'how much longer?'"

"Um, I don't remember." *Damn!* That thought wasn't meant to be vocalized. Her face flushed with heat.

Mac pulled out and sat back on his haunches. His eyebrows knit together. "Is this a bad time for you, Angie? I mean, we can make love another time if this is inconvenient." Sarcasm dripped from his voice.

"Oh, Mac, stop exaggerating." She lifted the sheet to cover her torso. "I wasn't going to orgasm anyway, so when you're done, we're done."

"What the fuck?" The tone in his voice rose. "This isn't a trip to the dentist, for Chrissake!" He ran a hand through his tousled hair and slapped his thigh.

"It's not like I can come in that position." The excuse sounded lame leaving her mouth, but she didn't know what else to say. She was having sex with him because, well, he was her husband and that's what *he* liked. She could take it or leave it.

"Why didn't you say something?" he implored.

The ceiling fan spun around on low, and the sheets were disheveled across the bed.

She shrugged a shoulder. Really, he was making a big deal out of nothing.

He got up and stomped off to the bathroom. She heard what sounded a lot like "son of a bitch."

Angie pursed her mouth and stared at the closed bathroom door, wondering if he'd return. She waited several moments and Mac didn't come out. Should she try to patch things up? She yanked the sheet closer across her body and nibbled her lip, uncertain.

Ignoring the growing pit in her stomach, she stood, slipped on her cotton robe, and stalked to the bathroom.

"Mac, do you want to talk about it?"

He splashed water on his face, and looked up at her through the mirror, his eyes cold. "No. I can't talk to you right now."

She licked her lips and walked to her nightstand to pick up the romance she'd been reading. If Mac was going to go off and sulk, she didn't need to stay. He'd cool down, eventually.

Thankfully, the boys were in bed, so that meant thirty minutes of peace and quiet. Maybe if she got engrossed in her book, she could push away what had happened tonight, at least for a little while.

She'd had to set the book down hours ago in order to start dinner, and the story was just getting hot.

Angelique MacKey had loved reading romance for years, but truthfully her interest had been reinvigorated as the distance and arguing with her husband, Steven "Mac" MacKey, had increased. They would argue over the simplest, most mundane things. Last week was the familiar fight over finances. She'd spent too much on the kids' sports equipment. She knew his pet peeve was not having his dry-cleaning back in time for a work meeting. Never mind the fact she'd spent the whole day in the car running errands and had two parent-teacher conferences he'd missed. It became aggravating, coupled with feeling taken for granted by Mac, she found herself avoiding him more and more. In and out of the bedroom.

Tonight, she'd worn a long satin nightgown, fluffed her hair, and refreshed her Chanel perfume. He had appreciated her efforts—as he always had in the bedroom—and it didn't take long before the gown lay in a pile on the carpet.

Then she had to open her big mouth. Brilliant.

She would need to apologize, and they'd have to talk about what happened. And God, she prayed it wouldn't turn into a yelling match, which seemed their typical *modus-operandi* as of late.

She sighed heavily when she sank down into a comfy chair and switched on the table lamp in the family room. She tucked her legs underneath her and opened the book to her marker.

The tasty novella she'd been reading told the story of a single woman seeing two men, and the woman had a hard time deciding between the two. The heroine and one of the men had just returned from dinner out, and Angie almost drooled knowing what would happen next.

Mike walked into her apartment and Jenni closed the door behind him, tossing her keys on the side table.

Smiling, she asked, "Would you like a drink?"

"Sure," he replied. "What do you have?"

Jenni strolled into the kitchen and called out her short inventory. "I have red or white wine," and opening the fridge, "or light beer. Which would you prefer?"

She leaned down to peer into the fridge and felt Mike's warm hands on her waist, gliding over her hips and behind. She straightened and closed the door as his lips strung sensual kisses up and down her neck. She angled her head to the side to give him better vantage. His tongue slicked over her skin and sent a shiver right through her.

Mike turned her and brought his lips to hers. The kiss started slowly and built to a simmered passion. Tongues tangled. His kisses left her breathless and achy.

He wrapped his arms around her waist fully, pulling her body into his very hard form. She reached up and crossed her arms around his neck. He stroked her back and behind with his hands. His tongue in her mouth made her melt. She leaned into him and moaned.

He broke the kiss long enough to whip her sweater off and then her bra.

Her breasts grew heavy, and her nipples peaked to hard nubs.

Returning his mouth to hers, he stroked and kneaded her breasts with one hand. He ran his thumb over her nipple, and she let out a little moan. He trailed his mouth down her neck, her chest, to her breast. His tongue played around her taut nipple but didn't touch it directly. He proceeded to the other breast, again ignoring the nipple. She arched her back up to him, wanting more. He kissed and licked all around, until she couldn't take it anymore.

"Mike, please." Her voice was barely a whisper.

He smiled against her skin but didn't keep her waiting. He put his mouth over her nipple and took it *in. He sucked hard, sending a sudden rush of throbbing heat to her sex. She gripped his shoulders and let out a cry. He did the same thing to the second breast. Jenni's sex grew wetter as the warmth spread throughout her body.*

Her heart rate sped, and for a brief moment, she imagined Dane's mouth over her nipple, sucking her until she begged for mercy. She enjoyed the shocking image of both Dane and Mike at her breasts. Mike moved his mouth lower, over her stomach. His hands worked her pants' button and zipper, pulling them and her panties to the floor. Instead of waiting for her to step out of her garments, he simply lifted her up and carried her stark naked to the dining table.

"Lie back," he commanded, then spread her legs apart.

He brought his lips to her stomach, dipping his tongue into her navel. His kisses passed her sex and went down the inside of her thighs. Then he separated her swollen lips with his thumbs and gently blew a hot breath before he circled her clit with his tongue.

She moaned and gripped the edge of the table as Mike continued his pleasurable assault. He slipped one finger inside her and stroked slowly. God, the anticipation could kill her. He added a second finger. She felt her climax build with demand. He continued with his tongue, gliding, licking, sucking. His fingers continued their ministrations, and Jenni froze with the pleasure building inside her, panting. Waiting for release. And then, as when the floodgates open after a storm, her climax thundered through her in a rush, leaving her boneless.

Mike shed his clothes double-time and sheathed his erection with a condom. He wrapped his big hands around her waist and slid her closer to him as he stood between her legs. He slipped inside with far more control than she expected.

Their gazes met and locked as he slowly pumped into her slick channel.

Keeping his eyes on her, he moved a finger to her mons, gently stroking the area, but never making contact with her clit. She licked her dry lips.

"Feet on the table," he directed.

She bent her knees and placed her heels on the edge, opening her up to him more. Mike's teasing brought a rush of moisture. God, she needed to come again.

"Tell me, Jenni. Does your other guy know how to fuck you like I can?"

She didn't say a word. She didn't show her surprise. She merely held his gaze. Never before had Mike asked about Dane. And frankly, Dane hadn't asked about him. She supposed it was only a matter of time. She didn't hide the fact she was seeing another man from either one of them. But she hadn't expected it to become a competition.

"And does he give you multiple orgasms?" he asked when his finger glossed over her clit.

"Ah!" She bowed off the table.

He took the opportunity to suck one taut nipple into his deliciously talented mouth. His finger continued, and his rhythm increased speed.

She shamelessly bucked up, meeting his every stroke. The tension built and she groaned until the bliss of another climax rocketed through her. She clenched down on his cock, igniting his own orgasm.

"Jenni," he grunted.

He collapsed over her, both of them panting with exertion.

He lifted his head after a few moments to look into her eyes. "Jenni, there's nothing I wouldn't do for you. I'm falling for you, and I'll do anything I can to prove to you that I'm the one you should be with."

Holy shit, Angie thought. Now that was some seriously amazing sex. A man who could wait for his girl to finish first. And Mike really wanted to be with Jenni; he really loved her. Geez.

Angie was beyond turned on after reading that scene.

Biting down on her lip, she snuck one hand under her robe and felt her pussy. Wet.

She quieted her breathing. Upstairs was completely hushed, not a peep. She hadn't heard anything but the air conditioner running. Glancing at the clock, she knew the kids—and her husband—were sound asleep.

Licking her lips, she closed her book and switched off the table lamp. The room went completely black with only bits of moonlight peeking in through the windows. She shifted in her seat, hooked a bent leg over the arm of the chair, and smoothed her finger down her sex.

She held back a moan as her eyelids fell closed. She circled and stroked and dipped inside. This was what she needed. Time to finish what she and Mac had started in the bedroom.

She pulled her robe open and arched into her hand.

"Mmm," she breathed as her nether lips and clitoris swelled. The heightened sensation built quickly. She was almost there, and she wasn't even trying that hard for it.

Oh so good. Within several short moments, her much-anticipated climax flew through her, making her body tremble in the chair. She sagged.

Wow. She spied the clock, and only five minutes had passed. Angie snorted. *That's* what her life was missing. Feeling alive.

CHAPTER
TWO

A ngie rolled out of bed early to get the boys off to school with as little upheaval as possible. Mac generally would sleep a little more, then get ready for work. Only after the kids were off, could she then take a shower. Sometimes to avoid being late for work, she'd put her makeup on in the car. Dumb move, but effective.

That morning, Mac didn't stay in bed. He headed right for the shower. The sound of slamming doors and drawers coming from their first-floor bedroom seemed louder than usual. He was pissy all morning, clearly still fuming about the prior night.

Whatever. He got to come *all* the other times. So *one* time he didn't come, and he acted like he had a stick up his ass. *Welcome to my world, bub.*

And you're kidding yourself to think that's the issue, Ang.

Well, they would move past this, like all the other times. She loved her husband, but there were definitely times when she didn't like him very much.

Time to check your pride. She walked into bathroom.

Mac stood in the closet, bare-chested, fastening his pants. She loved her husband. In fact, she and Mac had been love at first sight all those years ago when they'd met working for the same firm after college in Austin. He'd captivated her. Tall, dark, and handsome used to turn her on insantly. When he was around her, she could hardly string three words together. Love hit her like a bucket of ice water.

Seeing him naked used to make her knees weak and her mind fuzzy.

What happened?

"Mac, I want to apol—"

"I have a meeting later tonight," he cut in. "I need something from the dry cleaners. Can you pick up the laundry or is today too inconvenient?" he asked in a snarky tone in front of the bathroom mirror.

He couldn't even make direct eye contact with her, or bother to say please.

What the hell?

"What crawled up your butt and died?" Never mind. She didn't want him to answer that. "Yeah, I can pick up the dry cleaning," and with that she reached in to turn the shower on full blast. She spun around to strip. It was hard to hide anything in a room this small.

Mac always used to stand there and watch, with a devouring look on his face. Now, he only glanced her way once with complete disgust, and in a second, he was gone.

Angie stepped under the warm water and let it coat her naked body. Her breath escaped in a long exhale, one she hadn't realized she'd been holding.

Sure, she still loved him. He was a good provider, good father, mostly considerate, and an overall decent human being. Somewhere along the way, their relationship had changed. They argued more and had sex less.

Mac's climb up the corporate ladder required travel until he was gone easily seventy-percent of the time. Work was stressful, and that put him on edge, which took a toll on their communication.

Too often, she'd be cooped up in the house with the boys and be so excited to have Mac home so they could go out for dinner and a movie. She'd ask and he'd say, *I eat out all the time, Ang. The last thing I want is to eat out in restaurants.*

At some point in the last two years, Angie had quit asking and turned into herself. She found things that interested her. Not other men, although she'd had offers. She read more, spent more time shopping or meeting up with friends. She learned about Netflix and how all those wonderful shows she'd missed the first time around were now available at the push of a button. She was pretty good at marathon watching.

As a public relations exec, she leveraged her degree and steadily grew in her career, aided of course because she poured more into her work. The boys' lives, too. The good news was the boys thrived on the attention. Grades went up as did their social skills.

The bad news was Angie only felt more alone. She'd gained weight, and unless she was reading a steamy romance, had no interest in sex.

Since Mac's promotion six months ago, he was no longer traveling, and consequently, he spent more time at home. She hoped that would change things, bring them closer together. But the more time together only made them quarrel more often. He started to pick at her daily activities more, how it was too expensive, or pointing out all the things she hadn't done yet. And ignored everything she *had* done already.

She sighed as she scrubbed the shampoo out of her shoulder-length hair.

All of this reminiscing made her recall Mac's thirst for life that had invigorated her. Their trips before the kids were born. Her first time snow skiing had been with Mac. Together they were a force. He made her feel alive, and as a team they were unstoppable. She missed feeling that way. Feeling passionate. She missed what she and Mac once had. A stab of pain hit her heart, crippling her with sadness. Like she was mourning his death. In fact, she was mourning the loss of an amazing relationship.

Tears threatened to spill from her eyes. She quickly doused her entire face under the spray and rinsed. She needed to get her ass in gear and get to work.

Enough feeling sorry for yourself, Angie.

Mac drove to work as he had done since receiving his promotion to Chief Marketing Officer six months back. Only this time, his hands gripped the car's steering wheel hard enough to turn his knuckles white.

Dammit! Angie brought out a side in him he was not proud of. Mac generally maintained a level head and an even temper. Today that would be a challenge for him to manage.

What the hell happened last night?

Sex had been tapering between them over the past few years. Mac realized that happened with most married couples; it's to be expected. He'd believed, incorrectly it seems, that Angie was still relatively happy with their sex life. He would prefer having more sex, but took care of matters himself regularly to keep from constantly wanting to jump her. When they made love, he would have bet that she reached orgasm.

After last night, he wasn't so sure. And the thought ate at him. Why hadn't she said anything?

Stopped at a light, he ran his hand over his face and along his jawline. Thinking about it more, their relationship had changed over the years, and not in a positive way. They fought more than they ever had, and even as they tried to shield it from the boys, their sons knew what was going on.

Once, Mac had come home to a note left on the counter, a report from a parent-teacher conference. It seemed Robbie had made some inappropriate comments—comments that Mac himself had spoken.

Mac hated arguing with Angie.

Shit!

How could he fix this?

Chapter Three

A ngie arrived to work on time, thankfully, and was immediately met with the smell of donuts. She opened the desk drawer of her over-size cubicle and put away her purse. The cubicles were temporary until the fifth floor offices were finished with the remodeling.

"Morning, sunshine," Nicole greeted her from over their shared cubicle wall. Nicole was the quintessential morning person—up by four most mornings, ready to tackle the world. Of course, by eight at night her friend and coworker was useless.

Angie smiled to herself remembering how she'd learned that interesting fact years ago when they'd all gone out for drinks one night after work. Nicole practically needed to be carried home at the end of the evening—not drunk, but tired.

"Morning. Do I smell donuts?" she asked.

"Yup. Tina's birthday is today. She's not here yet. Quick, sign the card." Nicole handed over a cheery card in a peach envelope.

"I completely forgot. I'm so glad you remembered. Thanks, Nicci." She signed with a flourish and returned the card to her friend.

"You alright? You seem a little off today."

If anyone would notice something was off, it would be Nicole. She had a sixth sense about people. In addition to the two of them being friends for years, not much got past her.

"I had a rough sleep. Nothing more coffee can't fix, I'm sure."

"Hmm. Let's go out to lunch today."

"Sure. And keep those donuts away from me. I don't need the calories."

Nicole chuckled and spun around, returning to her work.

The morning flew by. Angie worked public relations for a high-end women's clothing boutique company called l'Amour Lux. The Dallas-based company owned more than a hundred stores throughout the US and Canada. The plans for next quarter called for testing a handful of stores with a men's line. The buzz in the industry thus far was mixed. Some critics believed l'Amour could pull it off, others seemed less certain.

Angie had her work cut out for her. For the past several months, she'd met with designers, buyers, merchandisers, sales managers, and of course the executives of l'Amour. The official press release wouldn't go out for another thirty days, but anyone who might be quoted in a paper, magazine, or website about the move would need to be coached.

Angie also needed to prep the executives who would be hosting the press conference. She rolled her eyes at that thought. When l'Amour did something, they went big. She recalled the time they'd expanded into Canada. The company president, Pierre Jarmon, a five-nine, French fireball, wanted as much fanfare, hype, and drama over the event as possible. The company hosted a "launch party" at the Ritz-Carlton in Toronto. Angie used every persuasion technique she could comfortably use to convince Pierre *not* to have the city close down the street in front of the hotel.

She still chuckled over Pierre's disappointment. *But Angelique, this is the event of the century. There will be hundreds of people at la partie, and thousands trying to crash it. Beyoncé et Jay Z will be there.*

Nicci's voice broke through Angie's thoughts. "Ready for some lunch?"

Angie glanced at her watch. *Where did the time go?* "Yeah, let me save this doc and we'll take off."

Nicole had been a long-time friend of Angie's since two jobs prior. In fact, Angie had been instrumental in getting Nicole a job with l'Amour. Nicole worked in operations while Angie managed a team of four people in public relations; however, they ultimately reported up through the same channel. Over the years they'd grown as close as sisters.

They stepped outside in the Texas heat, although September was the beginning of the cool down, and Angie slipped on her sunglasses. She and Nicole strolled to the sandwich shop two blocks east of their building.

They ordered and took a seat as they waited for their number to be called.

"So, why do you seem a little down? You and Mac have another fight?" Nicole started.

Angie sighed. "No, not exactly, although he was giving me the passive-aggressive treatment this morning, barely speaking to me."

"What happened?"

She bit her lip between her teeth. "I might have said something that offended him."

Right then, their number was announced and Nicole popped up to retrieve their tray of food.

Placing their plates down, then taking a seat, Nicole asked, "What did you say?"

"We were having sex last night—"

"Good for you," Nicole interjected.

Angie gave a half-smile. "My mind wandered . . . to my to-do list and groceries, and I think I said something out loud."

Nicole raised her eyebrows.

"I may have said, 'how much longer.'"

"Oh, shit." Nicole's face fell. Nicci was a realistic optimist. She usually wore a smile on her face, and her laughter always caused her hazel eyes to crinkle at the corners. Some people claimed she could be mistaken for Sela Ward.

"Yeah. Ya got that right." Angie took a bite of her turkey and avocado sandwich. "It just came out. Of course, he didn't get to come, but neither did I," she whispered.

"You were bored. You need excitement, Angie."

"I know," she shook her head in shame.

"Baby, have you told him what you like? What turns you on and makes you come?"

This wasn't the first time they'd had an intimate conversation out in public like this, and Angie was eternally grateful for the noise in the restaurant so they couldn't be overheard.

"Yes, but I don't think it registers. I don't know, I guess I'm not comfortable talking about it. Now, I'm to the point where I just want to get it over with. Get in, get out, be done."

Nicole gave her a breathy laugh. "This isn't your well-woman checkup."

Angie shrugged a shoulder, and swallowed hard before leaning closer to Nicole. "It's not the same as it once was, Nicci. I almost wonder why we're together. I think Mac and I have grown apart."

Nicci set down her glass of iced tea. "You're not thinking about leaving him, are you?"

Angie's eyes rounded. "I don't know." She exhaled.

"No, I actually haven't thought about it until this very moment."

"Have you thought about seeing a counselor?"

"I brought it up to Mac once. You know him. 'I'm too busy to meet with some shrink.'" He was the epitome of stubborn.

"Maybe *you* should go. By yourself."

"I've thought about that," she nodded slightly, picking a tiny morsel of meat off her plate. "This morning, I looked at him dressing for work, and do you know what I thought? Nothing about how handsome or sexy he was, nothing about any kind of affection for him. I felt angry at him. Angry for missing our sons' parent-teacher conferences again. Angry for yelling at me over his damn dry cleaning."

"Do you still love him?"

Angie looked up from her half-eaten sandwich. Mac put work before her, took her for granted, and seemed to find giving her what she wanted in the relationship a challenge. But even still, she could only think of him as her husband. "I do. I don't like him sometimes, but I still love him."

"Well, there's your answer." Nicole cupped her hand over Angie's. "There is enough there to salvage. To build on. Going by yourself, it may just take longer, but you can do this. Y'all have been together for twenty years. Don't throw it all away until you've exhausted all your possibilities."

Angie nodded and gave a shy smile. She didn't want to

leave Mac, and Nicole had some great points. Definitely something she would need to sleep on.

Nicole's advice had always been spot-on. Nicole was just a year older than Angie at forty-five, married to the same man for almost twenty years, and had a wealth of wisdom. The difference was she and her husband had a more laid-back relationship than Angie and Mac. They rarely argued. They were "peas n' carrots" while she and Mac were more "oil and water."

She'd think more on it later—right now, she had to wrap up work and get to the dry cleaners.

Mac took a seat across from the president and CEO of Frisco Snack Company, Raymond Criswell, in the executive lunchroom. The lunchroom was more like a restaurant, one floor below Mac's office. They served breakfast and lunch, and upon request, could have dinner available. As convenient as it was, he usually appreciated getting away, even if he ate by himself.

Mac had a feeling this wouldn't be a short lunch when he noticed George from R&D already seated at the table.

"George. Ray," he said by way of greeting.

"Hey, Mac."

"Mac. George. I brought you both here to review the plan for wrapping up the quarter," Ray started.

Mac nearly groaned. Hadn't it been discussed to death? Numbers were down year-over-year, but with some new additions to their healthy snack line, projections showed to finish the year up.

The trio ordered from the waitress, then Ray opened a spreadsheet on his tablet and continued, "I like the numbers from the recent test marketing of the new baked potato chip products. Mac, we discussed expanded distribution, and this is just the kind of product to finally get us into Mama Oats and Freshie's grocery stores. How are we looking on that front?"

"I've got sales teams calling on both of those chains. They are excited and committed to carrying the products in select stores in the hopes of a rollout nationwide. I expect purchase orders within the next three or four weeks."

Mac knew his numbers. Frisco would have their new products in other health food stores as well as conventional stores. He knew what advertising dollars were needed to launch the new products, how many stores they'd be in, and the approximate revenue the new products would generate before year-end. He knew the manufacturing costs, too. The rising costs worried Mac, and why the VP of Manufacturing wasn't at that meeting surprised and disappointed Mac.

"And you think this rollout will provide enough bump to grow the bottom line? Wall Street will be looking for that."

"I do." Mac nodded once. "I'm meeting with Camille later today to review the projections. We could expect a four or five percent bump over last year."

Camille Ferguson, the Chief Financial Officer, was the reason Mac had to work late tonight. She'd told him she was booked and after hours was her only availability this week. Of course, after last night and the morning he had, Mac wasn't anxious to get home.

"Great," and as if sensing his earlier question, Ray answered it. "Unfortunately, Will couldn't be here to address the manufacturing cost projections. I'll be meeting with him tomorrow morning first thing," his lips thinned, "and we can see what's going on over there."

Ray flipped the page and brought out another sheet with notes printed on it. "Now, George, let's review the five new products and the plans for follow-on products into next year."

Mac's mind wandered as he dug into his salad. Truthfully, he may have been in no rush to get home, but it was unavoidable. He would need to face Angie sometime. He was angry, but mostly disappointed, but hell if he knew what he was going to say.

CHAPTER FOUR

Angie hung the dry cleaning in the closet, and went to the kitchen to start dinner. She had about an hour before picking up Stuart from football practice.

Thirty minutes later, she had dinner ready. "Robbie!" she called, and he scampered down the stairs. Without being told, he washed his hands and set the table for four.

"Dad's working late, so it's you and me, kid," she said placing two full plates of spaghetti down.

Robbie dug in immediately. Angie smiled to herself. Robbie had his dad's eyes and nose, and no doubt, with his voracious appetite, would be tall like Mac. "Did you get yourself a snack after school?"

"Yeah," Robbie said, not stopping to let conversation interfere with eating.

"So, what happened in school today?"

He paused with his fork midway to his mouth. "What do you mean?" he asked, his brows knitted together.

She looked across the table. "I just meant, how is school? Anything interesting going on?"

"Nah. Nothing really. Got an A on my math quiz. It was mostly review stuff from last year," he managed to get out in between forkfuls of pasta.

"Excellent. How was English today?"

"Good. We had a sub," he smiled indulgently.

She rolled her eyes at him. Robbie didn't seem to be too impressed with his English teacher. He thought Mrs. Farmer was tougher on the boy students than she was on the girls. Considering they were in the first few weeks of school yet, this was something Angie wanted to keep an eye on, if only to be a sounding-board for Robbie's frustrations.

"Okay, so how much more homework do you have?"

"Not too much," he replied, "but I need to study for a science quiz tomorrow."

He'd nearly finished his dinner, while Angie was only halfway through. "Do you want more?"

"No, I'm good. I'm going back upstairs." He stood and stacked his plate and fork in the dishwasher. "I'll have dessert later."

"I'm leaving in about fifteen minutes to pick up Stuart. Your dad should be home at any time," she called after him.

"Okay."

Having said the words aloud, she couldn't say for sure when Mac would be home. In the six months since his promotion, he didn't work late many nights, so she didn't have much history to go on. She paused her chewing. *Is he really working late?*

33

She truly didn't believe Mac would cheat on her, but they said most women missed the signs. Either that or they chose not to see them. Angie felt her lip tremble.

In all their years together, she'd never suspected infidelity. But honestly, Mac was a good-looking man. She'd always known that. And at forty-six, he looked better than ever.

Angie had been hit on before. What was the chance Mac had been hit on too? Maybe by some woman he worked with? Very likely. And what was the chance he flirted back?

Was it possible he, like her, was having obligatory sex at home, but exploring his wild and crazy side with another woman?

Suddenly, she lost her appetite. She scraped the remains of her dinner in the trash and loaded the dishwasher.

Crap! She wouldn't generally label herself the jealous type, but her mind reeled now. Had she missed something? Was there something else going on behind all these arguments?

Mac sat in his office, reviewing spreadsheets, while he waited for Camille. Filling the screen before him, he glanced over the budget for advertising and couponing, funds for operations, and incentives for distributors.

With a light rap on the door jamb, Camille announced her arrival. "Hey, Mac."

"Hi, Camille. Come on in."

"Sorry about needing to meet so late. With three weeks left in the quarter, I'm slammed," she said with a sigh, giving him a half-smile.

"I understand. Have a seat." He gestured to the empty chair across from his desk.

Camille had the look of a curvy 1950s Swedish movie star. She stood about six-foot in her heels, and although she was in her mid-forties, she could easily be mistaken for a woman ten years younger.

She sat, set her notebook on the corner of his desk and crossed her legs, showing off her shapely calves.

Camille had never been married, which Mac couldn't understand. She was friendly, smart, and very attractive.

Mac pivoted his monitor toward the center so they both could view the screen at the same time. They hammered through the numbers for advertising which included print, Internet radio, and airport and train station billboards. He already had a crew working on the social media blitz.

"Do you have the timetable for the radio and print spots?"

"Yes." He flipped a few keys on the keyboard and brought the document to the forefront. "These are the numbers for next month and projections for subsequent months," he said while he pointed to each column.

Camille covered Mac's hand and slid it down two rows,

his finger sliding down the screen. "What's that?"

Her move surprised him. Why hadn't she just pointed? Mac maintained a neutral expression. "Um, that's strictly print ads that include a coupon."

"Okay. Great. Can you print that out for me?"

"Sure," he replied and sent the document to the printer.

She stood, glided to the credenza next to Mac's desk, and kept her back turned to him as she reviewed the sheet.

It struck him as odd when she didn't return to the chair. Did she linger on purpose—intending to give him a view of her backside? He furrowed his brows.

"Okay, great." She spun around and took her seat. "Can you go back to the original sheet?"

With a few keystrokes, he returned to the budget and pricing document.

"I don't see any numbers for vending." She tilted her head and bit her lip.

Camille appeared more . . . relaxed than usual. Her focus was still on business, but something felt more casual with her. Mac couldn't say *why* she was different; he just couldn't recall a time during their four years working together when she'd been like this.

"That's right. Initially, we won't place the new products in vending. I want to get a feel for how manufacturing could impact the numbers."

She nodded slowly. "You're concerned unless

production costs come down, it won't be worth it to even have these available in vending machines. Or . . . snack bars?"

"That's right."

She returned to studying the screen. Perhaps Mac had acted hastily in his assessment of Camille. She had a good head on her shoulders. The strain of working long hours could be taking its toll on her demeanor, but that certainly wasn't a crime.

They continued to discuss distribution, and the timing of product placement with advertising. They agreed to meet the following week to review some more numbers, but essentially they were both in agreement that the new products' launch would add to Frisco's bottom line and provide a decent boost to profitability.

On the drive to his home in the Dallas suburbs, his head swam. Camille acting casually, even . . . flirty with him. A rise in manufacturing costs hindered a full-blown product launch. And last but not least, Angie. The woman he'd known for twenty years suddenly seemed not to enjoy sex anymore. She was having sex with him out of obligation? He groaned aloud.

He stopped the car in front of their house, watching through the front window, and trying to recognize the woman he married all those years ago. Asking himself what had changed in her.

He entered his house to the usual amount of evening

chaos—mostly Stuart picking on Robbie, and Angie trying to bring it to an end.

"Hi, Dad," Stuart called from behind a forkful of food.

"Hi, Dad." Robbie lifted his eyes momentarily from his phone.

"Hi, guys. What's going on?" Mac asked cautiously as he hooked his suit jacket on the back of a chair and yanked off his tie.

"You hungry?" Angie called from the kitchen.

He nodded. "Yes." The salad from lunch wasn't enough to last him until eight at night.

"Dad, our game Friday night is away. We play Pearson. Can you make it?"

"Absolutely," he replied as he rolled up his sleeves and washed his hands at the kitchen sink.

Angie placed his plate in front of him, and returned to cleaning up the kitchen. He took a seat and dug in. Mac glanced up at one point and noticed Angie walking out the front door with a pot in her hand. That was interesting.

Stuart spoke what Mac was thinking. "Mom, what are you doing?" he asked when she returned, wearing a sassy grin on his face.

"I tossed the water from the steamed broccoli on my flower pots. No sense throwing it down the drain," she said matter-of-factly.

"Mom, you're a weirdo," he said playfully. Stuart was usually the more serious of the two boys, but every once in while he made surprisingly humorous or witty comments that only showed his genuine and softer side.

Robbie chuckled from the family room. She tipped her head to the side and scrunched her face into a snarky smile. Mac dropped his head, facing his plate, to hide his smile.

After dinner, Mac relaxed in his favorite recliner with the tablet on his lap and the TV remote in his hand. He switched to a show he, Angie, and Robbie would enjoy. Stuart headed to his room to work on his homework.

Angie strode in, standing in front of the recliner, her lips thinned in a straight line. "Curriculum night is next Tuesday at seven o'clock. It would be really great if you could make it this time, Mac." Then she spun around and leaned down to give Robbie a kiss on the forehead. "Good night."

"G'night, Mom."

Mac frowned. Dammit! He wanted to talk to her. He couldn't talk that morning because he'd needed time to formulate his thoughts. They were on a downward spiral as a couple. Anymore, they had more bad days than good.

Frankly, he was frustrated. Angie had changed. She wasn't the same woman he'd asked out twenty years ago.

She complained of being either too tired or too busy to want to do anything together when he was home from being on the road. She looked pretty—had always been—but it seemed like she didn't care about her looks much anymore. Her dress was always impeccable for work, but at home, she wore stuff like old sweats and faded T-shirts. She'd gained some weight, too. And they didn't talk much anymore. He remembered early on in their marriage, they'd sit after dinner, polish off a bottle of wine, and talk. They'd talk about anything and everything. She was more than his wife; she was his best friend. Maybe still his best friend. At that exact moment, he couldn't say.

Angie awoke the next morning and turned to see Mac asleep on the other side of their king-size bed. Despite going to bed early the night before, she hadn't slept that well. Too much on her mind apparently, specifically how to move past this hostility, and how to trust that her husband wasn't cheating on her.

She couldn't stop herself, she had to know—one way or another. With soft footsteps, she went into the closet and lifted Mac's shirt from the laundry basket to her nose. It smelled like only his cologne. She then walked to the home office where his phone sat in the charger. She tried several combinations, trying to unlock the screen. No luck. She hunted for restaurant or store receipts or anything that might be out of the ordinary. Nothing.

She sighed. If he *was* having an affair, he covered his tracks well.

After she helped Robbie find his English notebook, and confirmed what time to pick up Stuart from football practice, she headed for the shower.

"I think we're avoiding what happened the other night," Mac said as he walked into the master bathroom.

Her breath hitched. "You scared me." She hung her dress on the hook and turned his direction.

"I'm sorry." He said it, but she didn't feel the sincerity in his words. "I think we need to discuss what happened."

"What would you like to say?" She asked that stupid question to buy time because she didn't know what she wanted to say. *Yes, Mac. Sex is tired and boring anymore. It's all about you. I'm just a depository.* But she knew even in her anxiety that was no way to handle it.

"Angie. What is going on with you? Do you not like sex anymore? Frankly, I don't buy it." He stood in the doorway, wearing the boxers he'd slept in, a hand on his hip. His brown hair disheveled, his eyes had a look she'd never seen before. Concern or frustration? Maybe a bit of sorrow.

Seeing his naked chest, taut muscles, and broad shoulders, used to make her breath hitch. Now she felt nothing. "Mac, are you having an affair?"

His eyes rounded. "Am I having an affair? No. Absolutely not. Should I be asking you the same question?"

God, she was so tired. Tired of discussing everything to death. Tired of arguing. Over stupid stuff like their pitiful, cramped bathroom. Tired of being unhappy, and likely depressed. Tired of wanting things to be different and always being disappointed. "Mac, it's not the same. *We're* not the same."

He ran his fingers through his hair and let out a frustrated sigh. "I know that. All couples go through ups and downs—"

"For how many years, though? When was the last time we had an 'up'?"

"I don't know the answer to that." He looked like she felt—sad, depressed, defeated.

"We should see a—"

"Don't say it, Angie." His hand cut through the air like he had made the final decision. Judge and jury.

"I want a divorce," she blurted.

"What?" Mac's eyes widened with disbelief.

CHAPTER FIVE

A ngie swallowed past the lump in her throat. She hadn't meant to say it. Really. The words hung between them like thick black smoke, and she had a hard time taking it back. Mac simply stared at her with stunned eyes.

Her brain registered what he'd asked. Although, from the look on his face, he'd heard exactly what she said. "I want a divorce," she repeated.

The words felt easier to say the second time.

The more seconds that passed, the less . . . hesitant she felt. The statement had shocked her, but at the same time, a calm, liberating feeling swept over her. Like a weight she'd been carrying for God knew how long had suddenly lifted from her shoulders.

She took in a breath.

"I can't fucking believe this." He scrubbed a hand over his face and held her gaze.

"Believe it," she said in a cool, rational tone. A tone she'd used when an employee had made a wrong move, and she needed to make it known it should never happen again.

She wasn't sad. She wasn't angry. She was . . . relieved.

"Angie, we're going through a rough patch. We just need some time."

"No. We really don't, Mac. We've given it years. I've been wanting to see a marriage counselor for years, and you keep dismissing it, like *I'm* not worth your time anymore. Everything I've tried hasn't worked, and you can't be *bothered* to fix it with me. I'm done. We've stayed together for the sake of the boys, and enough is enough."

He looked down and shook his head in denial.

They had nothing more to say. She forced herself to strip and get in the shower. They'd need to keep up routine for the boys. She had to continue on with work, otherwise she'd crumble.

Angie stepped out of the bathroom forty-five minutes later, and entered the kitchen.

Mac wasn't at the table drinking coffee.

He was gone.

A divorce? That was the last thing Mac expected to hear from Angie. He thought they would argue, blow off some steam, then after things calmed down, they would return to normal. *What a fucking mess.*

He slammed a drawer closed on his desk. The clank echoed through the office.

How long had she been thinking about this? She wasn't

having an affair, was she? He stared at his bookshelves blindly. With his traveling, she certainly would have had the opportunity. Now that he was grounded, maybe that put the kibosh on her escapades.

Shit!

A knock at the door broke his stream of thought. Camille stood in the doorway in a red dress, high heels, and a bright smile. "Sorry to interrupt. Criswell wants to see us in his office. I think Will Manning is in there now."

Mac pinched his brows. Why would Ray want him in a meeting with the VP of Manufacturing? "Thanks. I'll be right there."

She lingered a bit longer watching him close up his PC and slip on his jacket. He caught her stare. She smiled and spun around to leave.

What the hell was that about? Camille had acted strangely around him as of late, and he had no earthly idea why.

He strode down the hall to Criswell's office to see the others seated around the table.

"Please join us, Mac," Ray called.

Mac took a chair and tried to get comfortable. Tried to appear normal, unaffected, and focused. But everything felt forced.

Camille passed him a copy of the financial data that pertained to manufacturing. Frisco had three manufacturing facilities—one in Dallas, one in Mexico, and one in Spain.

Will continued what he'd been saying before Mac entered. "The problem is everything has gone up. Wages have gone up. Add to that the energy cost increases and raw goods . . ." he trailed off. Shaking his head, he said in a low tone, "We should consider raising our prices."

"We can't pass those increases on to the consumer. Or we'll be higher than our competitors," Camille quickly interjected as she pursed her lips.

Mac pinched his fingers over the bridge of his nose. A headache started pulsing behind his eyebrows. He took a drink of water from the glass placed in front of him.

"Will, we've talked about this last month. We need to find a way to bring these costs down." Ray stabbed the spreadsheet on the table with his finger. "They're close to being out of control."

Mac took another drink, a bigger one, and the image of Angie feeding the cooking water on the household plants the previous night came to mind.

Water. The word popped into his head, and then out his mouth. "Water," he said under his breath.

Everyone stopped and looked at Mac.

He stared at his glass. The idea rolled around in his head, formulating.

"What was that?" Ray asked.

He raised his sight to Ray, then to Will. "Water. We need to cut our costs for water."

Mac leaned forward in his chair and focused on the financial data in front of him. Geez! The amount they were spending on water alone was atrocious.

"What about water?" Will asked with a sigh. The man didn't want to be in that meeting any more than Mac did.

"We are spending insane amounts each month on water. Multiply that by three. What if we recycle the water used in manufacturing? I mean," he shrugged a shoulder, "how many gallons do we use in washing the potatoes for potato chips?"

Ray's brow peaked, and Will's eyes narrowed.

"I'd need to look it up, but I imagine several thousand gallons a month," Will answered.

"Exactly. There must be some way to capture what we need, filter it, and reuse it. If a water treatment plant can do it, then so can we. We just need to do it on a smaller scale."

He glanced around the table. Clearly, the minds were calculating. Camille looked brightly at him.

"Mac, that could work." She faced Ray. "There would be some initial capital investment, I'm sure, for equipment, but Mac's idea has merit."

"Maybe we try it here, then roll it out to Spain and Mexico later. Once we get the processes nailed down, determine maintenance costs," Mac added.

"What do you think, Will? Could something like that work?" Ray asked.

Will tipped his head back and forth, as if mentally

working out the logistics of the plan. "It could."

"Let's do some research, people. Get a team together Camille, Will. This could save us boatloads of money."

"Not to mention, it's a smart thing for the environment," Camille chimed in and slanted a look of approval toward Mac.

"Right. Maybe even look into a packaging recycling program, if we continue of this 'going green' initiative." Ray stood. "Alright. Everyone get to work. Good job, Mac. I want to review findings a week from today." He patted Mac on the back once. His boss wasn't much for flowery accolades, so that simple gesture spoke volumes.

As they filed out of Ray's office, Camille leaned in closer to Mac. "Great idea." She smiled generously before sauntering passed him down the hall.

Will stuck out his hand. "Thanks, Mac. I'll let you know what I find out," he said, relief in his tone. No doubt, he'd been in fear of losing his job. This one thing could save the company tens of thousands of dollars. Enough to stave off a retail price hike.

So there it was. Mac stroked the back of his neck. Today was potentially the best day of his career, while simultaneously the worst day of his life. He made it back to his office, slumped in his chair, and stared out the window of the twenty-sixth floor office at downtown Dallas.

What the fuck am I going to do?

After the boys went upstairs to finish their homework, Angie pulled sheets and a blanket from the closet and began making up the futon in the office.

"What the hell are you doing?"

Angie's heart hitched as she spun around to face Mac, standing in the doorway. She inhaled. "Shit. I'm making up the futon so you can sleep here."

His eyes narrowed, studying her for long seconds. "This isn't like you, Angie. What's changed? Are you seeing someone? Is that where this is coming from?"

She stood upright, her face growing warm. *How dare he?* "Seriously? No, I'm not. I have a full-time career, take care of the house, cook and clean, do all the boys' stuff." She slapped a hand over her chest. "Sure, I'm having an affair in all my spare time." She wanted to cry, she wanted to scream. "But I'm sure you've had plenty of opportunity with all the traveling or working late. Anything *you'd* care to share?"

She waited a beat, and when she didn't hear an answer, she stormed passed him to grab his pillow off the bed.

He followed her. "I told you. I'm not having an affair. But I think you're being selfish."

"Excuse me?"

"Do you seriously want to put the boys through this?"

A bead of sweat trickled down the back of her neck. "Don't put this all on me. Here," she flung his pillow at him. "I was selfishly making your bed, but you're a big boy. You can handle it on your own."

God bless it! She stormed to the bathroom, slamming the door closed behind her.

She wouldn't cry. She would *not* cry. Although her eyes clouded in spite of her commands. She leaned against the vanity and tried to calm her racing heart. A flood of emotions hit her—anger, pain, sadness—and she hadn't a clue how to deal with them.

She washed her face and got ready for bed. It was too early, but she was exhausted. She opened the bathroom door, just as Mac had pulled on it from the other side. She met his gaze.

His eyes locked with hers, then he quickly took a step back, waiting for her to pass first.

She awkwardly passed and headed for bed. She could hear him gather a few things, and shortly after the door opened and closed.

She lay in the darkness, wondering if she would make it through this divorce alive.

Chapter
Six

A few days after her and Mac's explosion, Angie had an appointment with an attorney specializing in divorce. She glanced at her watch as she sat in the waiting room, fidgeting with the piece. Her foot swung restlessly.

"Mrs. MacKey, please come in." Sherrill Monahan offered her hand.

"Thank you."

"I understand you want to file for divorce." Sherrill took her seat behind her desk and looked Angie directly in the eyes.

Hearing it out loud was no less strange than a two-headed dog offering her a martini. She swallowed hard. "That's correct."

"Okay. I want to ask first, is there any hope of a reconciliation? Have you tried counseling?"

Aside from a few days ago, the last time Angie had asked Mac if he would consider counseling was at the end of last year. Stress in the house had been high. She'd obviously picked the wrong time to broach the subject. His company was trying to close out the year strong, and he was still traveling Mondays through Fridays. But his promotion was right around the corner, and Angie held on to hope that things would soon change because Mac'd become more apathetic at home. Some nights he'd fall asleep on the couch. Angie'd noticed he started tuning out to television, and sometimes the kids. Mac was clearly overworked. She should have expected his reply: *I barely have time to brush my teeth. There is no way I have time to see a shrink.*

"My husband has no interest in counseling. He believes he's done no wrong. So, no, reconciliation is not an option."

She nodded once. "I see."

Sherrill explained that she strove for a collaborative divorce and what that meant. She also discussed her fee structure, and after they agreed on that, she started asking Angie a slew of questions to get the suit filed.

She also recommended Angie contact a financial advisor, if she hadn't already. "No matter how badly you want this over, you need to be smart," Sherrill advised.

Then she explained how mediation worked and asked that any requests go through her instead of directly through Mac.

They finished up, and Angie walked out of the building feeling like she was wading through fog. She slid into the driver's seat of her car and sat for several moments. She could do this. She *had* to do this. She was miserable the way things were, and this was her only way out.

Her diamond ring stared back at her on her left hand. Sparkles danced off the light. She twirled it around her finger, the warmth of the band mocking the coldness of their relationship. She slipped it off, and stuck it in the interior pocket of her purse. Her hand looked strange now. Naked.

Move on, Angie.

She ignored the nauseous feeling in her stomach and finished her day at the office. Work provided a fine distraction. When Nicole stood to leave, she asked, "Nicci, do you have a minute?"

"For you, always." Nicole swung around the cubicle walls to Angie's cubicle. She grabbed a chair from an empty space and sat down, her face placid. "What's going on, Ang?"

"I asked Mac for a divorce a few days ago."

Nicci remained silent for a moment. "I'm sorry."

Angie exhaled and stared down at her hands. "It just came out, but frankly I didn't have the motivation to take it back. In some ways, it felt liberating to say it," she said in a calm, but sad tone. "I dread telling the boys."

"I bet."

"Mac is still in the house, although he's sleeping in the home office."

"How long will that go on?"

Angie shook her head. "Not long, as far as I'm concerned. I suspect he's looking for an apartment."

Nicole nodded. "So, how are you doing?"

"I think I'm okay. It's just so . . . surreal. Like this really isn't happening. I'll wake up at any moment and realize it was all a dream." She smoothed her lips between her teeth. "When we first got married, I never envisioned this for our future. I saw us growing old together, still making each other laugh, holding hands when we walk, and kissing each other goodnight. I certainly didn't envision arguing about how much money was spent on eating out last month or why I couldn't do *at least one load of laundry every day."*

Her eyes clouded.

Nicole leaned in closer, holding her hands. "Take it one day at a time, babe. You'll get through this. And of course, I'm always here for you."

She gave her friend a half-smile before they hugged. Nicci was her best friend, and having someone who cared and would listen was all she could ask for. She bit back the tears; there would be time for that later.

Angie knew she'd erected a wall around her heart. She used to be so laid-back and carefree. Years of disappointment made her callous, and she hated that about herself. But building a wall was the only thing she could think to do to survive, to manage every blessed hour of every day.

Mac noticed Angie's missing wedding ring from her finger the bloody minute he walked through the door. A knife to the heart would be less painful.

"Where are the boys?" he asked as Angie stood wiping down the kitchen counter.

"Upstairs, doing homework." She glanced briefly at him. "Your dinner is in the oven."

"Thank you," he replied while he pulled against his tie, slipping it off and loosening another button.

Shit. Was this how they remained calm and non-defensive—talk in simple, short sentences? Like they were practically strangers.

She hung up the washcloth, dried her hands, and looked at him. "We need to talk to the boys."

He nodded. "When?"

"Now. We should get it over with, so you can find an apartment and move out."

Her words stung, but he wasn't overly surprised by them. He'd already been on the hunt for an apartment. Hearing the words spoken, though, added to the complete picture of chaos, disappointment, and emptiness he'd been feeling. He knew once he got through this bullshit, he'd be stronger in the end. But that was little consolation now.

"And they will stay here."

She nodded. "We need to let them know we are going to work out arrangements so that we can co-parent, and we shouldn't throw around any accusations."

Did she direct that statement to him? His eyes narrowed. "I agree."

Her facial expression hadn't changed one bit since he'd walked in. He found it impossible to read her thoughts.

They called the boys downstairs, and everyone took a seat around the kitchen table.

"We need to tell you boys something," he began.

"Your father and I are getting a divorce," she cut in.

Both sets of eyes widened, and Robbie's mouth gaped.

"Please know we love you both, and this has nothing to do with you." He couldn't even tell if any of his words were registering with them. "This is not your fault."

"If we could have worked it out, we would have," Angie added. "Your father will find an apartment, but he'll be close. You'll stay in the house with me, and we'll figure out arrangements for you two to see him regularly."

The silence that fell on the room was bleak.

Finally, Stuart spoke. "I should have figured since Dad was staying in the office the last few nights."

Angie nodded. Robbie's eyes watered, but Mac could see him feverishly blinking back the tears.

He covered Robbie's hand with his own. "We'll get through this, guys. We'll be better in the long run."

Robbie pulled his hand back, and Stuart snorted.

Okay, they just needed some time to adjust to the news. As any child would. Hell, he was still *adjusting*.

"What about our games?" Robbie asked, his face twisted in grief. "You're not going to come anymore? You're supposed to help coach next season." His eyes pleaded with

Mac.

She cleared her throat. "We'll try and keep the schedules as normal as possible. Your dad will still come to your games; he just won't live in this house anymore."

Mac threw a glance her way. Her words were certainly innocuous enough, but he couldn't help wonder if there was some hidden meaning to them. She never took her gaze off the boys. He noticed her eyes appeared misty as well.

"Is there anything else?" Stuart huffed.

"No. Do you have any questions?" Mac looked at them one at a time.

They both shook their heads.

Mac caught sight of Angie twisting her hands in her lap. "Okay. You can always come to us if you do. For now, you're excused," she said.

They rose and double-timed it back upstairs. Before Mac could say anything to Angie, she'd stood and turned to make her way back to the bedroom.

"Okay," he said to no one. He strode to the bedroom. "Angie, I really don't think this is the best option. I'm willing to see a counselor with you, if that's what you want. But ending it, . . . well, there's got to be a way to fix this."

She met his gaze for several long seconds, and he thought maybe, he'd broken through.

"Mac, you need to find an apartment, and do your own cooking and cleaning. That's a fix that I can live with. Now I'm going to get ready for bed."

She walked into the bathroom, closing the door. Telling him, the conversation was over. He thought of following her, but he didn't want to risk another argument. Instead, he left and went to the kitchen.

The quiet in the house was unnerving. These are the times when a man needs a dog, he thought.

Mac pulled his dinner from the oven, poured a glass of wine, and sat back down. Damn, the meatloaf was excellent. Angie was a good cook. Actually, she *became* a good cook. He could recall more than one occasion when dinner was burned or tasted foul because she'd screwed up the recipe. He laughed to himself.

Now it would be his turn to learn to cook.

He groaned and forked another bite.

CHAPTER SEVEN

A ngie and Mac had decided it would be best not to have the boys present when he moved out. Serendipitously, both boys had practice for their sports Saturday morning. Angie hadn't returned yet from dropping them off. What was taking her so long?

His gut wrenched. He'd planned on talking with her before leaving. Maybe to avoid leaving. Give it one more try, in *their* home. The whole week had been short, *polite* communication. But basically a lot of avoidance. Avoiding each other and avoiding talking about how to fix them.

Is this what it boils down to?

He slammed shut an empty dresser drawer. Eyeing a framed photo of the two of them shortly after getting married, he lifted it out of the box and set it in the middle of the dresser.

How could someone throw twenty years away?

He wouldn't give up though. He would find a way to win Angie back. He hadn't a clue on how, but damn! There had to be a way.

Mac carried another box to his car and slammed the trunk closed. He'd packed a fair amount of his clothes, some dress shoes and workout shoes. He boxed some casual clothes, toiletries, and his alarm clock. Although the apartment was furnished, he had no doubt he would still need a few things. Glancing around the house, he reached for a framed picture of the boys taken at the beach and another of all of them celebrating Angie's birthday a few years back.

He roamed the kitchen. Really nothing there he needed.

He took in a shaky breath and turned to leave.

He was stalling. And he knew it. *Where the hell was she?*

Angie dropped off the boys for their practices and started for home, but never quite made it. She'd driven the back way into the neighborhood and parked under a huge, shady oak tree several houses away.

She could see that the garage door was open with Mac's car still parked inside. He hadn't left yet.

Her breath hitched when she saw movement.

Mac put his suitcase in the backseat, then opened the driver's side door to sit. Soon the brake lights switched on and the car backed out of the garage.

Her breath stalled in her lungs as he pulled out of the driveway, moved up the street in the opposite direction of where she'd parked, and out of the neighborhood.

She sat for long moments, watching even after he was out of sight. Vehicles had passed, but she didn't care. She started her car after a few beats and pulled into the garage. Walking into the house, Angie heard nothing. The silence felt eerie. The house had a new kind of emptiness. Angie shivered as she glanced around.

Snap out of it! You wanted this.

Angie straightened her back and walked into the bedroom. She slipped off her shoes and got to work on her weekend chores. She put on the radio, hoping to kill the absolute silence of the place until the boys got home.

Stripping the bed of its sheets, she went upstairs to do the same in the boys' rooms.

Whew! Some room deodorizer might be in order.

She loaded the washing machine and returned to the master bedroom for more to wash. She walked into the closet and froze.

Mac's side of the closet was half bare. Blank bar space and a few stray hangers sent her head into a tizzy. She hadn't prepared herself for that.

She took a deep breath and reached into the hamper for dirty clothes. Some of Mac's clothes lay on top. Tears welled in her eyes. She lifted out the laundry and left the closet. A framed picture of the two of them as newlyweds caught her attention. Mac left it there intentionally. She stared at the happy couple. She wanted to warn that couple everything isn't rosy; marriage required a crap-ton of work.

She made a half-step toward the door when she collapsed to her knees on the floor of her bedroom. A sob escaped.

She shook her head as if she couldn't understand what was happening. What she was feeling? She wanted this. Asked for this. *Did you seriously think it was going to be easy?*

Didn't people say that? "Divorce is the easy way out." Hardly. This was anything but easy.

More tears streamed down her cheeks. Hunched over the laundry in her lap, smelling the vague scent of Mac's cologne, she couldn't move from the spot.

A radio station aired a song that sounded vaguely familiar to Angie. She lifted her head and tried to focus. Lisa Stansfield's *All Woman*—a song about a man taking his wife for granted. No truer words were ever spoken.

She struggled to her feet, leaving the pile of clothes behind and went to the radio, staring at the miserable thing. At the end of the song, the man came around and the relationship was saved.

Thoughts of her and Mac's time together flooded her mind. Twenty years later and he still wasn't "coming around."

"Ah!" Leaning down, she yelled at the device, a tiny bit of spit flew. She picked up the radio with two hands and yanked the cord from the wall, causing the lamp to jostle.

Her face grew hot.

"Ah!" she yelled again as she lifted it over her head and threw it to the ground.

Expecting the device to crash in a million pieces, it only bounced and rolled twice on the plush carpet. *Dammit!*

Tears streamed down her face as she just stared at her vacant room. Funny, it always seemed too small. The whole house seemed too damn small. But not today. How many times had she just needed room for herself? Suddenly there was plenty.

Rubbing her hand over her aching heart, more tears streamed down. *How can I ease the pain?*

She let out a loud breath, realizing all this nonsense would get her nowhere. She wiped her eyes, bent down to retrieve the laundry, and made up her mind. She would have a productive day. No matter what.

Damn you, Mac.

Mac dropped his luggage and shifted his hanging baggage to slip the key in the apartment door and open it. He strode into the solitary space and looked around. There was a neutral-colored sofa and upholstered chair with a coffee table in the living room which spilled into an eating area and the kitchen. The whole space looked like different shades of beige and brown.

A stark contrast to the reds and yellows in his house. Angie had done the bedroom in pale blue and gold; she'd called it "spa blue."

This is home for a while, he thought, before he hefted his bags to take them to the master bedroom. He made a few more trips from his car, bringing in boxes, bags, and his golf clubs. He stowed most of it in drawers and closets, and finally dropped down on the sofa for a breather.

The apartment was just a place to keep his things and sleep, and had a bedroom with two twin beds for the boys. It was conveniently located halfway between the house and work.

It wasn't *home*. The whole damn thing felt unreal, like he was living someone else's life. The lives of absentee fathers, take-out dinners, and work-obsessed men depicted in the Lifetime movies Angie watched, which all led to broken homes. He rubbed a hand over his brow.

Time to focus on something else. He stood and went to scope out the kitchen. Most of what he needed in terms of cooking implements appeared to be there, but nothing edible beyond several gratis water bottles the management company left in the fridge. What he really needed right now was beer.

He swiped his car keys off the counter and made his way out.

After an hour of shopping for the essentials, beer, and a take-n-bake pizza, he returned to the apartment. He sent out a few texts to his close friends, inquiring about their evening. Considering it was a Saturday, he had a chance of getting in on a poker game or watching a college ball game. In no time, a few guys got back to him that they already had plans and wanted a raincheck. Ryan replied that he was out of town, but promised they would get together soon.

He opened his notebook at the kitchen table and popped the cap off his bottle of beer. Maybe he could get some sales reporting done.

He knew he needed to reach out to his boys. He worried, but damn if he knew what to say. He shot them some texts and got a few responses about hanging out with friends. Good for them. They should be around their friends during this time.

Geez! It was too damn quiet.

His home had been a hotbed of activity, of energy. He grinned. There had always been something going on. Boys coming and going. Friends showing up. Angie bustling about. Doing her own thing, either with the house or work, and keeping up with the boys' stuff too.

She was damn good at her job, always had a strong work ethic. Somehow she managed to have an incredible career and raise two incredible boys at the same time.

Angie.

What happened? What went wrong? How had he missed the cues? If Angie had been unhappy for so long, why didn't she tell him? He absently toyed with a pen, and replayed so many scenes they had together. Sure they argued, but didn't all couples? Even now, he could feel the heat fill his cheeks thinking about some of their disagreements. Most of them seemed so petty, in retrospect. No one was perfect. And they'd had good times, too. Like family vacations, sharing milestones when the boys were little, going on drives to look at the fall colors and picking up a gallon of apple cider along the way.

At least he'd *thought* they were good times.

They would not throw away twenty years. He shook his head.

Mac prided himself on being a solution-finder. There had to be a solution to this mess. His moving out could *not* be the final chapter in their relationship.

He loved his wife. In his heart of hearts, he had to believe she loved him too and would see that they could work this out. That this was merely a pothole in the road.

CHAPTER EIGHT

She had survived the weekend without Mac. She only thought about him a million times when awake and half a million when she tried to sleep.

Another day, another press release, Angie begrudgingly thought. At least when she walked in the office Monday morning, she knew she had work to distract her.

"Hey," Nicci called from over their shared wall. "How was your weekend?"

"It was fine."

"I thought you would call me," Nicci said, not in an accusatory way, but in a supportive way.

"I thought about it more than once, but I got through. The good news is my house has never been cleaner." She gave a sardonic grin, and Nicci smiled.

Angie turned back to her computer to focus on her busy day. She opened her calendar and saw several meetings scheduled. One with the distribution and marketing folks regarding a full rollout the men's line, another with several store managers about an outreach program they were a part of in California. However first, Terri in Advertising wanted to discuss a fashion campaign leveraging social media. Seeing her friend would be good; she missed Terri.

As she got comfortable in a chair across the desk in Terri's office, she glanced around at several large blow-ups of the latest ad campaign resting on easels. Angie reflected on how close the two of them used to be. Clearly, as the company grew, they got busier with their jobs and responsibilities, and life took its toll on their close relationship. In addition, Terri had gone through a divorce two years prior, and consequentially seemed to put herself in a cocoon.

Angie's heart had broken when she'd heard the news of Terri's divorce, but to make things worse, she'd felt pity for Terri. How ironic that she was now in that same position.

"Hi, Terri. You look good," she smiled at her friend. Terri had let her blonde hair grow passed her shoulders a few inches, but the color hid any gray trying to poke through. Her svelte body was just as Angie remembered it— statuesque with subtle curves.

"Hey, Angie. Thanks. I'm coming along. How are you?"

Angie smoothed her lips together and took in a breath. "Well, things have been better. I . . . was actually hoping we could talk over lunch. Are you free this week?"

Terri tipped her head, then turned to look at her

calendar on the computer. "Yes. Tomorrow, actually. Lunch it is. It's been a while," her voice dipped.

She nodded. "It has. So tell me your idea."

"Okay. I want your opinion before I run this by the team. If you don't think this will fly, then we scrap it."

"Okay," Angie said slowly.

"I would like to start a campaign on social media, a contest really, centered on the fashion of the stars. How often have we seen actors, royalty, etcetera," she waved her hand absently, "step out in hideous attire? Then they're splashed across the tabloids and picked apart on cable TV."

Angie chuckled softly. "It's true."

"Well, I want to hold a contest in which entrants send in the original photo clip of the star poorly dressed, and then a picture of how they would change it. Sort of a *before and after*." She paused a moment searching Angie's eyes for a hint of what she thought. "We could have prizes for first, second, and third place. What do you think?"

Terri had creativity running through her veins. No doubt about it. This *could* be brilliant. "Terri, I like the idea, but I have some reservations."

She sent a flick of finger pointing Angie's way. "I thought you might."

"On one hand, we get some great exposure, and really leverage our social media channels. On the other hand, we could be insulting some of the very folks that shop our stores. Not to mention, this probably wouldn't draw in our target market."

Terri pinched her lips together. "Right. One thing I considered was limiting the number of things that can be changed from the *before*. That would be like saying 'they were so close.' Would that minimize the insult-factor?"

"It could." Angie toggled her head side to side, thinking about how to spin this into a positive for l'Amour. It was a good idea; there had to be a way they could use it. "What if we target students and make the prize scholarship money. Then there would be less complaining," she said with air quotes, "because it benefits a really good cause—education."

"Yeah," Terri drew out the word. "Plus we hit our *future* target market."

"Do you have a budget?" Angie tapped her pen against her index finger.

"Not specifically. I thought I would formulate an idea with the team and generate a plan before I ran it up the flagpole."

"Well, obviously the bigger the prize money the more exposure and press it could gain for l'Amour." Angie raised an eyebrow. "But too high, and it could look too much like taking advantage of an unfortunate choice."

"True," Terri said with a smirk on her face.

Thinking through the plan, Angie said, "I can help with the positioning and messaging. Being a fashion retail company, this could show how dedicated l'Amour is to good fashion, furthering innovation in the industry, and educating future generations, Ter."

"We're on the same page. Great." Terri clapped her hands together. "I'll get my team working on a plan and the pitch."

"Okay, and if you want, run it by me before Jarmon sees it," she said with a smile, "but Terri, I love the idea. It's liable to go viral."

"I can only hope." Terri's eyes twinkled with enthusiasm.

Angie chuckled as she stood. "Okay, lunch tomorrow."

"You got it, Ang."

Angie made her way back to her office. Terri was a visionary, so creative. Terri used to call Angie to her office regularly to bandy ideas around. She hadn't heard from her friend in quite a while. Terri's divorce took a toll on her drive, and her outgoing nature. It was good to hear from her. Angie smiled. Good to see Terri's life getting back to some semblance of normal.

That thought dropped a pit in Angie's stomach. Did this mean *she* was doomed to have the same experience? Go through a battle to be free of pain and anguish only to enter into another world filled with pain and anguish? Angie let out a shaky breath. She couldn't think about it now; she might break down, and that was not good for business.

Mac shut down his computer and stashed some papers in his desk drawers. As he slipped his arms into his jacket,

Camille stood in his doorway.

"Hey, Mac," she said, wearing a bright smile.

"Hey, Camille. What's up?"

She strode in. "I'm sorry. Were you about to leave?"

"Yes. I have an appointment." Mac wanted to tear himself away early to meet with his attorney, Tyler Benson. He hadn't been looking forward to the meeting, but it was necessary nonetheless.

"Okay, I won't keep you. I was reviewing some revenue numbers for Australia. Sales seemed to have spiked considerably last month. Do you know why that was?" She tipped her head and her hair fell over her shoulder.

"Wasn't that right after the Outback Marathon? I think we were big sponsors this year, right?"

He *knew* they were one of the top sponsors of the marathon. He wanted to give Camille the benefit of the doubt. How unusual that she would ask him about this.

"Oh, that's right." She shook her head lightly and grinned. "I'm sorry to have bugged you. I probably could have found that out on my own."

He gave her a gracious smile. "No problem." Mac walked toward the door, holding the door knob.

Camille took her cue and walked out. She paused long enough to say, "Good luck with your appointment." She pivoted in her high heels and walked away.

That was odd, he thought. Granted he'd only been in this position six months, but Camille would have never come by his office for such a trivial matter. She would have called. He scowled. No, she would have gone to someone on her team first.

He didn't have time to deal with Camille right now.

Minutes later at his meeting with his attorney, they discussed a temporary order sent over by Angie's lawyer outlining custody of the boys, child support, and how the bills would get paid. Tyler had a great reputation, and Mac could see he was thorough. He even asked Mac if he thought Angie had a lover on the side. The thought turned over and over in Mac's mind. But his gut yelled *no way*. It wasn't in her make-up. He'd never had the sense she was cheating, even during all of his years traveling, he never thought she'd strayed. She emotionally pulled back, and that was frustrating enough.

His conclusion—highly unlikely.

All his travel, while good for his career, had been a disaster for his marriage. He vowed to not get consumed with work so much anymore.

"Okay. Let's go through some other items," Tyler said.

As they went through more details and discussed assets, Mac held back the rush of melancholy, and pushed aside the emotion that rose to the surface. He found himself wanting to give Angie what he could. He felt like he owed her. She was a good woman and mother. Perhaps she wasn't supposed to be a wife, his wife, but nevertheless, he didn't want the mother of his children to struggle.

His throat thickened as he spoke. "If divorce is imminent, I don't want to sell the house. In fact, there are only a few more years left on the mortgage, I should be able to pay it off." He didn't know exactly how Angie felt about the house, other than it being too small. Yet one thing he was certain of—she would want minimal disruption of the boys' lives. They *both* wanted that. And that meant keeping them in the house, at least until Robbie graduated from high school.

Tyler asked, "You said if divorce is imminent. You've been served with papers from your wife, Mac. How do you propose changing her mind?"

He paused before he answered. The man was probably going to think he was looney. "Honestly, Tyler, I don't know how—but I do know that I will find a way to get back together with her. She's my wife and always will be in my eyes."

Tyler had an excellent poker face. Mac couldn't be sure, but he might have seen a twinkle of admiration flash in the man's eyes.

On his way to the gym, Mac received a call from his VP of Sales, and personal friend, Cameron Blayke.

"Hey, Cameron. How's it going?"

"What—did you bail out early?"

Mac chuckled. "Yeah, man. I had an appointment."

"Alright. You free tomorrow night?"

"Yeah, sure."

"Cool. Let's grab a drink after work."

Mac liked the sound of that. Hanging with a friend was just what he needed to get his mind off his troubles, at least temporarily. "Sounds good to me."

"Okay. I'll probably see if Pete and Kurt are available too."

"Good idea. I'll see you tomorrow." He ended the call.

Whenever Mac was in town for the weekend from his travels, the four of them would play golf at the local courses. Mac missed his friends. Knowing he would see them again lifted his mood as he had something to look forward to.

He grabbed his gym bag from the trunk, strolled into the gym, and quickly changed. The first station he started on was the treadmill. He jogged up to a good clip, his goal being three miles. Only a few moments had passed when Bonnie approached him. Bonnie was a shameless flirt. Not even his wedding ring stopped her. That day she wore a hot-pink sports bra with blue stripes going down the sides, and tight shorts to match. The bra may have been a size too small because her enhanced breasts looked like they were stuffed into that thing.

"Hi, handsome. How's it hangin' today?"

"Good, Bonnie. How 'bout yourself?"

"If I were any better, there would need to be two of you to handle me."

Oh, yeah. She was a live wire. He let out a polite chuckle.

Then, in an unexpected move, Bonnie squeezed in alongside his treadmill and smoothed her hand down his forearm. "Lookin' good, Mac." Her exit—a more surprising move—was a pat on his ass. "Definitely looking good," she purred.

The smell of the sickly-sweet scent she wore lingered after she was gone. Bonnie meant no harm, but he was in no mood for games.

He jumped off the treadmill and slipped on his gloves. He needed to work off as much stress and frustration as he could, and one thing called to him to do just that. The punching bag.

Twenty minutes later and dripping with sweat, he snagged a towel and wiped his face. He grabbed some free weights to work his chest and triceps. Could he work himself to exhaustion? Possibly have a good night's sleep?

After a hundred crunches, Mac went to an area of the gym cleared for stretching out. More times than he could count, Mac had used strenuous workouts to help blow off steam, especially when he and Angie had fought. He knew for certain that although he'd had a tough workout, it barely dented his overwhelming frustration and helplessness.

The thought of failing Angie, failing their marriage, and letting his boys down, was more than Mac could face. He'd gone into his marriage thinking it was forever. There was no Plan B.

Although he wasn't perfect, he thought he'd done enough of the right things. Sure, Angie wanted more time with him, but traveling constantly didn't exactly make that easy. He'd call when he could though. And these last six months he thought was just adjustment. They would find a new groove and be happy again. It just took a little time.

Mac wiped the towel over his face and head. Clearly, the phone calls and gifts weren't enough. She had mentioned more than once that she liked it when he held her hand. He'd done that a few times, but didn't stick with it. Holding hands was a simple enough request. Wasn't it?

He exhaled hard. *Well, shit.*

A few more conversations replayed in Mac's mind. Requests she'd made. Tears of frustration she'd shed over his stubbornness. And that's what it came down to. He was stubborn . . . and stupid. The signs were there, and he'd chosen to ignore them. He took his wife for granted. Neither were perfect, but he needed to own his part.

The knot in his gut grew. A feeling of failure overtook him. He had to fix this.

If he did manage to win her back, a few things were going to change. He would listen to her, pay attention to her needs, compliment her more. And he was sure as shit going to make sure she came when they made love.

After twenty years together, he knew his wife's body better than her own doctor. She might have been faking it before, but with some patience, that would be a thing of the past.

All he needed to do was find an opportunity to show her he deserved a second chance.

CHAPTER NINE

Angie swung by Terri's office to pick her up for lunch. They opted for a restaurant within walking distance that was known for quality food and relaxing atmosphere, which was perfect for having a private conversation.

After twenty minutes of catching up on happenings in their lives, mostly surface stuff, Terri went straight for it. "So tell me, what's going on with you and Mac?"

Angie blotted her lips with the cloth napkin and placed it on her lap. "How perceptive you are." She gave her friend a small smile. "Actually, that's something I wanted to talk to you about. Mac and I are getting a divorce."

Terri reached across the round, wood table and covered Angie's hand with her own. "I'm sorry to hear that."

"Thank you. When I think about it, it's been in the works for years."

Terri nodded. "That's how I felt with Glenn. You don't go into a marriage expecting it to end."

"Exactly." She inhaled. "Now I'm sorta just getting through the days. I'd really like your advice."

Terri glanced up at the large group passing by, then focused back on her friend. "You're doing just what I would recommend at first. Take it day by day. Have you contacted an attorney?"

"Yes."

"I assume there's nothing there worth salvaging, and you don't think you could stay together for the kids?"

Angie's throat tightened, and she shook her head.

Terri's eyes read concern. "Do you want to talk about it?"

God, she couldn't say what she wanted. She wanted to talk sometimes. Sometimes not. She wanted to scream, and cry and have a pity-party. She glanced down at her plate. "I think Mac's years of traveling really took a toll on our relationship. Gone Monday through Friday, week after week, month after month. Then golf outings. I'd gotten so used to being alone," she shrugged her shoulder, "and lonely."

"Do you think he had an affair?"

"No, I don't. It would be easier, I think, being able to blame some random woman. But we grew apart and I didn't know how to reconnect. Ya' know? I'd try, like on our ten-year anniversary, I had a romantic getaway planned at a hotel. Mom was going to watch the kids. But Mac was called away for work. I'd plan a few other things and want to go out, but, I don't know," she shrugged her shoulders, "maybe I didn't try hard enough. Because later on in the relationship, when Mac did want to go out, I wasn't interested."

Terri nodded.

"Now with his promotion, he doesn't travel, but we can't seem to get back in sync. It got to the point where we were arguing so much, it's exhausting. So then I'd retreat, and he'd retreat . . ." She sighed. "Frankly, we were having more bad days than good."

Terri's sad eyes showed she knew just what Angie was going through.

Angie pushed aside her water glass and tended closer. "Terri, do you want to tell me what happened between you and Glenn?"

"We were very much like you and Mac. The distance grew between us, and we didn't know how to fix it. When I heard about the first affair . . ."

Angie silenced her gasp.

". . . I suggested we go to counseling. I quickly learned that counseling only works if both people are willing to try. Not too much longer, I realized he was a serial cheater."

"Oh, Terri."

She grimaced. "I'd heard once that men in the gas and oil business make pro sports players look like Mother Teresa."

"I am so sorry."

Terri took a sip of her tea. "Thank you. It turned ugly quickly. He lowered the credit limit on my credit card, basically cleaned out our bank account, and got nasty leveraging the kids." She looked up from her lunch. "Try not to let it get bad, Angie."

"Thanks, Terri."

"Each day gets a little easier. It just happens slowly, so hang in there. Take it one day at a time."

They finished lunch, and although Angie lost her appetite, she forced the last of her pasta salad down. She and Terri committed to staying in touch. Terri promised to be there for her, whenever she needed a listening ear or a shoulder to cry on. Knowing she had her long-time friend in her corner helped ease the ache in her heart just a bit.

They hugged goodbye and went their separate ways at work.

Angie knew she had a long, emotional road ahead. She'd have to take it one step at a time like Terri said. Deep down she wished she didn't have to go through this, yet she just didn't see another option. Terri words nagged at her. Would Mac turn into the vengeful ex-husband? Put her through the kind of crap Terri's ex-husband did. Would he play hardball in a divorce?

Did she have much choice in the matter? She was miserable with Mac, and miserable without him.

Cameron and Pete were already at Xavier's when Mac walked in. Mac watched the waitress approach their high table when Cam caught sight of him and waved.

Mac strode through the upscale bar, conveniently located two blocks from his office. The owners pumped a ton of cash into the place—polished hardwood floors, shelf upon shelf of gleaming liquor bottles, and a mahogany bar that probably cost a year's worth of mortgage payments.

"My man. Glad you could make," Pete greeted him with a quick hug and an exuberant smile. Pete was the shortest of the group, but with his sense of humor, his wife fell hook line and sinker.

"How's it going?" Mac asked them both and shook Cam's hand.

"We just ordered a round of beers and tequila shots," Cam said. Cameron took off his jacket to hook over the back of his barstool. The way his shirt pulled over his arm muscles showed his stocky build.

"Oh, he's ready to let loose." Mac looked Pete's way with raised eyebrows.

Pete shook his head and grinned.

"So, how's it goin', Pete? Haven't seen you in a while."

"It's good. Work got crazy, but things are settling down now. How 'bout you? What's new in your world?"

Before Mac could answer, Kurt stepped up to the table. "Dudes. So good to see your ugly faces." He hugged his friends and shook hands.

"Ugly? Speak for yourself. You're the oldest." Pete slapped him on the back.

Drinks arrived and everyone got comfortable on the

barstools. Conversation started with the usual bull—who was closing more deals, whose handicap had improved, and when the hell was Kurt ever gonna settle down like the rest of them. Kurt could have any woman he wanted—charming, good-looking, million-dollar smile—but he had little interest in settling down.

Mac knew he would need to share his news, but it would keep. The libations were flowing and so was the laughter. He didn't want to spoil it.

He turned to ask the waitress for another round when out of the corner of his eye he spied Camille walking in their direction, wearing a deep purple skirt suit with a low-cut blouse.

Mac rarely saw Camille outside of work. And as she walked in alone, it occurred to Mac that he rarely saw Camille with a man.

Every year Frisco would hold a company picnic, and maybe twice Camille had brought a guest, but that's it. She'd otherwise make an appearance, make sure all the executives saw her, then she'd leave.

How strange that she's here now.

She stopped at the space between Mac and Cam. "Hello Mac, Cameron. How are you gentlemen doing tonight?"

Both Pete and Kurt went slack-jawed, their eyes glued on Camille.

"Hello, Camille," Mac acknowledged her.

"Camille, this is Pete and Kurt."

Each man rose, and she reached across the little table to shake hands.

"Nice to meet you," she said with a smile.

"Likewise." Kurt's smile was unrestrained. "Care to join us?"

Mac wanted to kick Kurt under the table. And would if he thought he could get away with it. This night was for the guys. For drinking and cussing and shooting the shit.

"No, but thanks for the lovely offer. I'm meeting a friend." She rested a hand on Mac's shoulder. "I'll leave you to enjoy your evening." She pivoted Mac's direction. "So great seeing you outside of work, Mac." She smiled, then sauntered over to a table by a window with two other women already seated—four pairs of eyes tracking her.

"Holy mother of God. Would you two care to tell me who that beauty was and why neither of you ever thought to introduce me before tonight?" Kurt glared from Mac and Cam and back again.

"I'm happily married. I have no idea what you're talking about," Cam replied before lifting his beer mug.

"And you?" Kurt jutted his chin Mac's direction.

He raised his hands in surrender. "I'm actually surprised to see her here." He wrinkled his brow. "I rarely see her outside of work."

"Yeah. Odd, huh?" Cam chimed in.

"Well, before this night is through, I'm gonna have her

digits."

"Good for you and your one-track mind." Cam patted Kurt on the back.

"You slackers are just jealous because I'm the only one not married. I'm still gettin' some anytime I want it."

"Gettin' some VD," Pete said into his beer.

Mac smirked, and Cameron laughed.

"Yeah. Yeah. Laugh all you want. You know I'm right."

"Actually, about that." Mac knew there would never be a time he'd be comfortable telling his friends his wife wanted a divorce.

All eyes trained on him.

"Angie said she wants a divorce. I moved out Saturday."

The expletives flew.

Cam cupped his hand over Mac's forearm. "Shit, Mac. I had no idea. What are you gonna do?"

"What can I do? I should have seen it. We've been arguing on and off for a while." *Mostly on.* "And I still love her, but maybe she doesn't feel the same way."

Pete looked over at him. "Let us know if there is anything we can do. Anything at all."

Mac nodded. "Thanks, guys. Now let's not let this put a damper on the evening. Kurt, when the hell are the Stars gonna recruit some real talent?"

Kurt grinned at the ribbing. "You ass. We have real talent, but I can tell you this. We've got some up and coming talent from Kansas City I've got my eye on . . ."

Kurt continued talking about hockey and recruitment; Mac lost his focus.

Mac was glad he'd told his friends, but every time he talked about moving out or divorce, it felt all the more real. That scared the crap out of him. The more time he spent away from Angie, the harder it might be to get her back.

Several times in the last few days, he'd replayed instances when she'd needed him, but he always had an excuse. He'd taken her for granted. Maybe this would be a good time to go see that counselor.

He had to find a way to show her he deserved a second chance.

CHAPTER TEN

"**W**oman, you need to make a change." Angie sighed and shook her head as she stared at her naked body in the bathroom mirror. The pooch of a stomach seemed to have grown in the last few weeks, which was ironic since she had no appetite. The circles under her eyes and pale skin tone had dissipated, but the lingering signs of depression were still there.

"Maybe this is a good time to join a gym," she said out loud.

She pushed open the closet door to retrieve something that could serve as a gym bag and loaded it with shorts, tank top, shoes and socks. Rummaging through her drawers, she found a sports bra. When was the last time she'd worn that thing?

Angie knew working out would be good for her, even if she wasn't much of a fan. She used to belong to a gym, but couldn't remember why she stopped going.

Oh, that's right.

As the boys' schedules had gotten busier, she found it

hard to fit in. Early on, she and Mac would work out together. But as his work got in the way . . .

How often work had gotten in the way of their relationship.

The story of their ten-year anniversary she'd told Terri popped in her head. Angie'd planned a hotel "vacation" downtown. She'd called her mom and arranged for her to babysit the boys for a weekend getaway. She had the room stocked with cheese and fruit, a few bottles of wine, roses and candles. She'd even shopped for sexy lingerie at Lucy May, her favorite online lingerie store. Everything had been perfect.

They were on the way to the hotel when Mac got a call. Something about a proposal for a big client in California that was under critical deadline. He'd turned the car around, dropped her off and went to the office. His apologies were sweet and appreciated, but looking back she thought maybe that was writing on the wall. Maybe that was the beginning of the end.

Her eyes grew misty, and she dabbed them with a finger. She couldn't start crying again when she was a minute from the office.

Keep it together, Ang.

The morning was so busy that Angie had no choice but to eat at her desk. At this pace, she'd have no energy to go to the gym after work.

"Hey."

Angie peered up at the adjoining cubicle. "Hey yourself. How'd it go?" Every so often, Nicci took the morning, sometimes the entire day, to take her mother to her doctors' visits.

"Good. That woman will outlive us all." Nicci grinned. "So, you look like you were doing some heavy thinking."

"I'm going to join a gym."

"Good for you."

"And I was thinking about how tired I am and wondered if I will even have the energy to work out." Angie grimaced.

Nicci rested her forearms on the top of the cube wall. "Well, some of that might be because of everything you're dealing with right now with Mac."

She nodded.

"Another thing could be your hormones are crashing. That can affect your energy level, as well as concentration, sleep, and sex drive." Nicci lifted an eyebrow. "You know I've been taking maca root for years. Maybe you should get some."

Nicci had suggested maca some time ago, and Angie clearly had forgotten about the supplement.

"You know, this is another reason why you're my best friend."

Nicci grinned like a proud feline. "I know. I can't help being brilliant."

And both women laughed. She actually laughed, probably for the first time since she'd told Mac she wanted a divorce. Maybe this proved that she was going to get through this entire mess after all. Just maybe.

It had been two weeks since Mac'd moved out, and it felt like two years. The boys were trying hard to hide their animosity, but she could feel it whenever they'd pick at each other or make some snide remark.

Angie bumped up the level on the elliptical. She considered making an appointment with their school counselors, to fill them in on the dramatic changes taking place at home. The teachers may not give any leniency, but she'd hope for understanding at the very least.

On the bright side, this was her fourth trip to the gym this week. She made a conscious effort to load her gym bag into the car every morning before leaving for work.

Grocery shopping started to take a different feel too. Angie focused on buying less processed food and more organic items. Slowly, she was noticing a difference.

A man had pushed his cart down the aisle and looked back at her as she pulled some fresh basil off the rack. She'd hid her smile, and her delight.

She glanced at the clock on her phone. Two-hours before kick-off. Robbie made her promise to take them to the game, although she already knew, he wouldn't be sitting with her. He'd be off with his friends in the student section.

She blotted her face with a towel and went to the ab machine.

Hopefully, Stuart would get some playing time tonight. He loved football too much to sit on the sideline.

Her phone vibrated. She glanced down at the screen to see a picture of her and Mac taken at a birthday dinner they'd had at a fine restaurant seven years ago. Looking at it now, she wondered why she'd never updated it.

She simply stared at the screen, biting on her lip, hoping to calm her racing heart. Why couldn't she answer? Finally, the phone went blank. She exhaled.

Then, his text flashed on the screen.

Are you taking Robbie to the game? I can bring him and Stuart home if you want to leave early.

She really didn't want to think about running into Mac at the football stadium. Every time she thought of him or saw him, her heart ached, her whole body ached.

If she left early it could minimize the time she'd see him, but on the flipside she might miss a play if the coach put Stuart in.

That's ok. I'll probably stay the whole game.

He replied instantly.

Ok. See you at the game.

Ugh! She blotted her face with a towel. *That's just what I wanted to avoid.*

But she knew better. There would be no avoiding Mac in the future. They had two children together who would graduate from high school, graduate from college, eventually get married and have children of their own.

How would she experience all of these milestones without him by her side?

Tears threatened to well in her eyes.

Don't do it! Don't breakdown at the gym.

She blotted her face again and lifted herself off the machine to go do lat pull-downs. For the remaining thirty minutes, she'd worked-over three muscle groups and then stretched out. She needed to head home, check on the boys, and get dinner started. As she turned the corner, she opened her water bottle to take a large swig.

Damn! She almost ran straight into someone. She jostled to the left, and water sloshed on her cheeks and in her eyes, and dribbled down her chin. Hands wrapped around her upper arms, preventing her falling.

"Sorry." She wiped her face and opened her eyes.

"Angie?"

Shit! Mac stood before her in his suit with a gym bag flung over his shoulder. "Are you alright?"

She instinctively stepped back, her brain searching to piece together the scene. He worked out here?

If she didn't know him, she would do a double take. Mac wore his suit straight from the office—his jacket open and his tie loose. He exuded confidence and that made him equally sexy and handsome.

"I . . . I'm fine. I didn't see you."

His hands released her. "It's alright. I didn't know you joined the gym."

"Yeah. Just recently."

His eyes scanned her body, and he looked like he had something more to say, but decided against it.

Unease settled in her core. Being this close to him, and at the same time feeling like a stranger, she had to get distance. "Well, have a good workout." She backed away, and continued until she could break eye contact and turn to leave, careful to watch where she was going.

"Take care," he called after her.

She made it out the front doors and let out a breath she'd been holding in. *Gees! How awkward.*

One day at a time, she replayed Terri's words in her head. That would be her motto to get her through this mess.

CHAPTER ELEVEN

T he following day, Mac received a text from Ryan, inviting him to meet for drinks. He and Ryan were friends for several years now. And he was all too happy to accept.

As Mac walked into the bar, he saw Ryan stand to flag him down. Mac wend through the throng of people to his friend. Borrowed Money was a Dallas favorite and had the crowd to prove it. Briefly, he wondered if there was a chance he'd run into Angie.

"What's up, man?" Ryan grasped Mac's hand in a high handshake and leaned in to pat his back with his other hand.

"I'm hangin' in there. Could you have picked a more crowded place?"

Ryan rolled his eyes. "I don't know what's going on. This place is a zoo." He motioned for the padded stool next to him. "Turns out I can't stay too long anyway."

"Really?"

"Yeah, and I owe you an apology. I've been MIA these last few weeks. Work has been slammed and this traveling is kicking my ass."

Mac motioned for the bartender. "Heineken, please." He turned back to his friend. "I remember those days. A different city every week, or night sometimes."

"Yup. But I think I see the light at the end of the tunnel, now that third quarter has wrapped up for us."

Mac reached for his beer to take a swig.

"So what's new with you? Adjusting to the new position and all?"

Mac forced a smile. "I am, and it's going well. Life at home sucks though."

"Shit. What's going on?"

"Angie asked me for a divorce."

"No shit," Ryan said with a slump in his shoulders.

Mac shook his head. "Came out of the clear blue. I mean, things have been touch and go between us for a while, but couples go through shit. I figured we'd make our way through with time."

"So what are you gonna do?"

"I've moved out. I'm going to give her some space and hope for the best. The boys are taking it hard, but what could I expect? Shit, Ryan. I had no idea marriage would be so hard. I work my ass off and come home . . . to what? No appreciation, just a bunch of wants and needs." He let out a sigh. "What about what *I* want? What *I* need?"

"I hear ya, man."

Even though he and Ryan were tight, Ryan didn't need

to hear him gripe. His loneliness at times was unbearable, but being with his good friend helped. Mac needed to change the subject because he was just bringing down Ryan *and* himself. "So, enough of my bitching. What's new in your world? How are Carol and the kids?"

"Good. They're all good. Actually, I just learned Billy has a slight case of dyslexia, so he gets time with a specialist at the school to help him . . ."

Ryan went on about his family and work, and Mac had to force himself not to tune out. He threw in an occasional *mmm-hmm* and *uh-huh*, but his mind wandered in the worst way. He needed to shake himself out of this funk.

Three drinks and an hour later, Ryan glanced at his phone. "Crap, I gotta get out of here. I've got the six a.m. flight out to Atlanta in the morning." He stood, tossed some bills on the bar, and emptied his glass.

Mac rose and took his hand. "No problem, man. I'm gonna finish my beer and head out myself."

"Okay. Great catching up. I'll have you over soon. We can throw steaks on the grill," he said with a smile.

"Count me in." He watched his friend grab his jacket and head for the door. Seeing Ryan again was good. The two men had been friends since college. And even as Mac had trouble staying focused, having his friend nearby was exactly what he needed.

Mac spun back around and leaned his forearms against the bar. He had half the bottle to go, but he was in no rush. He had nothing to go home to.

He glanced around a bit. The place had thinned out, and he noticed a woman at a table with two others watching him. He gave a polite nod and continued to scan the bar.

The woman had perfect white teeth and blonde hair pulled back from her face. He took note that she intentionally looked his way—not trying to break eye contact when their eyes met. Interesting.

He took another sip and focused his attention on the TV at the end of the bar televising a football game.

"Do you only drink beer?" he heard from behind.

He pivoted around, and the blonde stood before him in a tan suit with a navy blouse and navy heels. Mac couldn't help but notice that the suit hugged her curves in every good way.

Of course, it could be the alcohol clouding his vision.

"Excuse me?"

"I've watched you drink Heineken all night. Is that all you drink?"

She'd watched him? "What else is there?"

She raised a brow and her mouth curved. "Bourbon."

Well, shit. This striking woman had some spunk to her. "You drink bourbon?"

She made a show of rolling her eyes, then took the empty spot next to him and leaned into the bar. Mac briefly gleaned a look at her perfect heart-shaped ass. Shit! This woman was trouble, and the best thing he could do would be to high-tail it out of there.

"Henry." The bartender turned, walked toward them, and gave a nod.

She pointed to a brown bottle up three shelves. "Let's get two of that delicious bourbon for me and my friend here. Neat."

"You got it," he replied.

Double shit! He'd *intended* to ask for the bill.

"Victoria Hemming," she said as she stuck out her right hand for his.

Exchanging names. Did she really think she'd be hanging around long? "Look, Victoria. I was just about to close out my tab and head home—"

"Home to the little woman."

He watched as her sight traveled to his gold wedding band. Although Angie had taken off her ring, he wasn't there yet. Deep inside, he needed to hold onto the belief that they could get through this. Removing his ring would be like admitting defeat. The final nail in the coffin.

Sadly, no he wouldn't be going home to *the little woman.*

The bartender set down their drinks and walked away.

"Here," she handed him a glass. "Have a drink with me before you head out."

Mac's eyes traveled from her face to the glass, then back again. Okay, one drink. Because, hell, this was an excellent brand and it shouldn't go to waste.

"Alright," he said.

"To good drinks and good times." She clanked her glass against his softly.

That comment reminded him of something Angie would say. Angie had an amazing confidence to her. Victoria certainly didn't lack for self-confidence. Angie's sensuality was subtle, but not hidden. The woman before him knew she looked good and didn't apologize for how she owned it.

They both took sips, and Mac savored the long, slow burn of the bourbon sliding down his throat. Damn, he hadn't had a bourbon this good in years. Even traveling on an expense account, he didn't take the time to savor the little things like this. Angie had called him a workaholic, and maybe he was because he'd certainly gone too long missing something this fine.

Victoria gave him a sexy little smile. "Good, huh?"

"Top notch."

"Are you going to tell me your name, or do I have to guess? 'Cause that could take all night," she drew out the last two words.

Challenging, feisty vixen. "Steven MacKey," he said as he offered her his hand.

She slid her hand into his, gently grasping, and said, "Good to meet you, Steven." The corners of her perfectly formed lips curved. She held on a bit longer than necessary before releasing his hand.

She took the seat Ryan had vacated and asked, "What

do you do, Steven?"

She crossed her legs, forcing her skirt to hike higher up her naked thigh.

Alarm bells were sounding in Mac's head. This woman had one thing she was after. It would be in his best interest not to accept her offer. He and Angie may be separated, but they were still married.

He glanced at his watch. Finish the drink and leave. "I'm in marketing for Frisco."

"Really?" Her head tilted to the right. "Good company."

"Yes, it is. And what do you do, Victoria?"

"I'm a real estate agent."

Boy, if he had a dime for every realtor he knew.

"Commercial or residential real estate?"

"Residential. I've been in the business for over ten years."

He nodded. "And the couple you were sitting with? Clients?"

"They were fellow agents from my office. We drop in here on occasion for drinks after work."

More than occasionally, Mac would bet, considering she knew the bartender's name. "Are you good at what you do?"

Fuck! He hadn't meant to ask that. At least not the way she would likely take it.

One brow perked up and her eyes glinted. "Yes. I ask a

lot of questions. It's the best way to learn what my clients are looking for in a house. But I'm placing them in a community, not just a house, so I also learn what I can about their personalities, their hobbies and interests. Like discovering that one might like top-shelf bourbon," she purred.

His lips quirked, and he tipped his glass. "Touché."

She licked her lips and leaned closer to him, "So tell me, Steven, what are some other things that interest you?"

That position gave him a decent view of her cleavage and one red, lacy bra. Mac's cock gave a little jump and he willed it to stay down.

That was strictly a primal response and meant nothing.

The way her eyes dilated when she looked at him confirmed she had one thing on her mind. Hell, if he didn't leave this very damn minute—get far away from her—he was screwed from here to Timbuktu.

"Victoria, you're very attractive, and I have no doubt you've heard you're a beautiful woman. I regret that I must call it a night and make my way home."

She straightened in her chair, letting the smile on her face slip a fraction. "Of course. I understand. My friends have left. Would you mind escorting me to my car so I get there safely?"

He could do that. Walking alone in the dark would not be safe for her. "Sure."

He paid for their drinks, and she slipped her purse over her shoulder. He pushed open the door for her and followed her out.

"I'm just over in the parking garage. Second floor."

"Alright."

They walked, chatting mostly about the weather and the cooler temperatures finally rolling in. They arrived a few feet from her midsize SUV when she lost her footing and stumbled. Mac quickly reached out and caught hold of her arm to prevent her from falling.

"Geez! Thank you. I must remember not to wear these heels again if I'm going to drink." She smiled to make light of her action.

Victoria gripped his forearm and leaned down to slip off her shoes completely and carry them. The garage floor was mostly empty at this time of night, so they walked straight to her SUV. She hit the remote, opened the backdoor, and tossed the shoes on the floorboard along with her purse.

She turned around. "Thanks again for catching me, and thanks for walking me to my car." Her hand went to his chest, and Mac felt the slight dig of her nails like cat claws on his muscle. She lifted herself on her toes to place a kiss on his lips. Her lips were closed, but soft and warm against his. He didn't jerk away. His mind told him to, but his body wouldn't obey.

She lingered until slowly glossing her tongue over the

seam of his lips, as a feline meticulously licks her fur. When he opened fractionally, her tongue slipped inside and tested, searching for his. His body responded on its own and kissed her back. She tasted like bourbon and hot female.

Her hands grabbed the back of his neck as her whole body went flush to the front of his. He held on to her hips and inched her shirt upward feeling the soft, warm skin of her torso.

What was he doing? Shit!

He pulled away and dropped his hands. His heart beat like a drum, and his cock begged to be set free, but hell! He was married. He had to leave this woman. Now!

Victoria trained her eyes on his while she unbuttoned her jacket and slipped it off her shoulders. She flung it on the backseat.

Mac pursed his lips. She was relentless, which pissed him off. Truthfully, he was angry with himself for not turning and walking away.

"Well, good night, Victoria."

In a brazen move, her fingers went to work on the buttons of her blouse. His head darted around the garage. "What are you doing?" he scowled at her, but she didn't stop.

Her blouse was now entirely undone and hanging straight down.

Still watching him and perhaps trying to read his mind, she slowly opened the blouse, letting it fall off her shoulders.

Fuck!

Then she reached for his hand and pulled him closer, placing it on her full breast.

"I want you to touch me." She lifted his other hand and cupped it over her other lace-covered breast. "I've wanted it the moment you walked in that bar."

She'd been watching him the entire time. The alcohol seemed to have disintegrated any remaining self-restraint he had. He grabbed the straps of her bra and yanked them down.

"Fuck." He massaged roughly at her moan, loving the power-play.

He wrapped an arm around her waist, hauling her up to him and his aching dick. He crashed his mouth over hers, their tongues collided and danced. Her arms flew around his neck, and she mewled into his mouth as she wiggled her torso into his raging erection.

She brought a hand to work on his tie and shirt buttons, but ditched that after mere moments to stroke his cock over his trousers. He groaned.

Her body was made for sin. And his dick wanted nothing more than to sink into the luscious body and hear her scream.

"In the car," she breathed over his lips as she worked his belt and pants button while pulling him to follow her into the backseat. She wasted no time unhooking her bra, throwing it to the floor, and hiking up her skirt. She lay before him, revealing her red lacy thong. She was a siren.

Her knee bent, resting her foot on the bench, giving him a view of her sweet pussy. Then she beckoned him with a wave of her finger.

"C'mere, Steven. I have a condom for that anaconda."

What?! He froze. What the hell was he doing?

Her eyebrows grew together. "Why are you stopping?"

Fuck! He tucked himself in and quickly zipped up his fly. "Victoria, I'm sorry. I can't do this."

She propped herself on her elbows. "But we were just getting started."

He barely heard her as he repeated, "I'm sorry," and closed the car door behind him. He jogged to the staircase, fixing his belt. He ran down the steps, out the street, where his car was parked.

His heart raced. Shit! What an asshole he was. What was he thinking? He was married, for the love of God. What came over him?

A wave a nausea threatened to have him spill the contents of his stomach. He braced his hands against the hood of his car, dipping his head. He took several deeps breaths and waited for the sensation to pass. Then, he flung the door open, started the car, and peeled out of the parking space as fast as he could.

"Fuck!" he let out as he slammed his fist against the steering wheel.

He had no business being with that woman, talking with that woman. She'd put on a full-court press, doing all she could to fracture his resolve. He wanted to work things out with his wife. And cheating was one sure-fire way to prevent that from happening.

He sped to his apartment, stripped out of his clothes, and jumped in the shower. He could not stop the thoughts that invaded his mind. The guilt he felt. He'd never cheated on his wife. Never had a desire to. Ever.

He'd seen the men hanging out in the hotel bars while traveling. They were kidding themselves to think they weren't inviting trouble. Mac would eat at the restaurant and make his way straight back to his room. Sure, he would have liked some company, chatting with the bartender or another businessman or woman, but it was too risky.

He saturated his head under the spray. All those years of minding himself—out the window in one night. One hour!

There was no choice. He had to tell Angie.

Are you a fool?

Shit! He didn't know what to do. He loved his wife, and the guilt of what he'd done to her bore down on him. He slammed his fist on the tile wall.

CHAPTER TWELVE

A ngie exited a conference room after meeting with the director of sales, conferencing in all the store managers, to review the communications plan for the new men's line when Patty rushed to her.

"Angie," she called.

Patty was a twenty-something curly-haired brunette with a sparkling personality. She never had a bad day, figuratively wore rose-colored glasses all the time. Which frankly was a good thing considering she was head of Customer Service. Not that l'Amour received very many complaints. Quite the opposite, but calls and emails still came in that needed to be addressed. Things like, why didn't they offer free tailoring services. Or could they find a sweater like such and such in a certain color. Or—one of her favorites—could lunch be catered at the store since one client in La Jolla liked to shop during her lunch hour.

"Hey, Patty. What's up?"

She looped her arm through Angie's as they walked side by side down the hall. "You know I'm not much into playing cupid," she started. *Oh, here it comes!* "But there is someone I want you to meet. I think you two would get along great."

Angie stopped walking and turned to face her friend. "I don't know, Patty. I think it's too early for me to be dating anyone—"

Patty held her hands up. "I know. I get that. Don't think of this as a date. Look, I told him all about you, and he can't wait to meet you."

"Patty," she exclaimed.

"Please don't be mad. He's very nice. He has no expectations, but I promise it will be worth your time. Think of it as free dinner." She gave shy smile.

Angie sighed aloud. *Oh geez!* "If I do this, will you promise to never try and fix me up with anyone else again?" she said in a firm tone.

"Yes, absolutely. His name is Bruce. Can I give him your cell number?"

She rolled her eyes. "You haven't already?"

Patty's smile brightened. "You won't regret this."

Angie had the distinct feeling she already did.

The next day, Angie's cell phone rang, a number she didn't recognize. Ugh! She hated telemarketing calls.

"This is Angie."

"Angie, hi. It's Bruce Livengood. A friend of Patty's."

"Yes. Hi, Bruce."

"Hi. So glad I got a hold of you. Patty's told me so much about you. I was hoping I might take you out to dinner, get to know you a bit more."

Crap! Her heart skipped a beat. She'd been separated just a few weeks. This could *not* be happening. "Bruce, I'm not sure if Patty told you, but I'm married." Geez, that was harsh.

"Separated. Yes, she had."

She sighed.

The tone in his voice lowered. "I understand what you must be going through. I've been divorced myself. I'm not looking for anything other than a quiet dinner, with delicious food and beautiful company."

Beautiful company? What did Patty say?

Maybe conversation with someone who'd been through what she'd been going through would be therapeutic. Maybe even speed the healing time or whatever. She sighed again.

"Okay, Bruce. But I'll meet you somewhere." She'd preferred not to have the boys see her going on a date, at least not yet.

"Sure, sounds great. How about next Friday night at Villa Richard. Say seven?"

Friday meant football games. "I can't do Friday nights. How is Saturday?"

"I need to leave town then. I can do next Thursday. Will that work?"

"Sure. That's fine."

"Great, Angie. I'm looking forward to it."

She sighed and stared at the phone for a moment before slipping it back in her bag. What had she gotten herself into?

Camille—who seemed to be making more personal visits than usual—rapped on his door. *Where the heck is Mimi?*

He waved her in as he sent an email to Dylan, one of his sales & marketing managers.

"I have the numbers from the water recycling study." She handed him the manila folder.

That he wanted to see.

She walked to the side of his desk to lean as he opened the folder. The document gave costs for equipment and installation, adjustments in the current manufacturing line—which weren't terrible—and water savings. His eyes rounded.

"Yup." Camille smiled. "Once we get this up and running in Dallas, we can save two-hundred million gallons of water next year alone." She pointed to the bottom of the report. "Then, once we do a full rollout we're looking at five hundred and eighty million gallons of water saved."

"This is unbelievable." He continued to scan. The report was thorough and seemed absolutely attainable once the equipment was brought online. "Incredible."

"You're incredible," she broke his focus.

He lifted his chin and faced her, not certain he'd heard her right.

"That was an incredible idea you had," she added. She motioned with her head. "That copy is yours. I'll keep you posted as I get more details." She slid her hand down his forearm, flashed him one last smile, and headed out to the hall.

Mac sat dumbfounded. Was it his imagination, or was Camille flirting with him? He didn't want to say anything just yet and embarrass them both. He'd give it some time, but he knew one thing for certain. Even if he couldn't get back together with Angie, an office affair was never a good idea.

He cringed at the thought of "an affair." The guilt over what happened with Victoria ate at him. And he had no idea how to fix it.

Currently, avoidance through excessive hours at the office, followed by strenuous working out at the gym, was his plan.

He stared out the window, a million thoughts racing through his head. Angie, and how the hell to win her back. Well, screwing around was a recipe for disaster.

And Camille. What the hell was up with her lately? They were business associates. That's it.

The epiphany hit Mac like a lightning bolt. For the first time, he had a clearer understanding of what women must deal with when they received unwanted advances. He personally followed the HR rules. It never crossed his mind to *not* treat a woman with respect. But on the same token, he knew some men would push the boundaries and even cross the line. Now, he recognized just how those women felt.

Well shit!

CHAPTER
THIRTEEN

At seven o'clock, Angie arrived at Villa Richard. She'd fed the boys and told them to finish their homework before any electronic use, not that they needed to be told. They didn't question her when she said she had a dinner meeting and would be home in a few hours.

Striding to the host stand, she said, "Hello. I'm meeting Bruce Livengood."

"Yes, ma'am. Right this way." The host greeted her with a nod and a polite smile.

Angie had been to Villa Richard before, years ago, with Mac. The restaurant offered some of the finest prime steak and seafood Dallas had to offer, definitely five-star. Following the host, she took in the richly-appointed space— dimly lit, with cloth napkins, wineglasses at every table, and floor-to-ceiling drapes on the windows. She briefly wondered if the art pieces were originals or reproductions.

She arrived at the table, and Bruce rose, adjusting the shirt cuffs under his jacket.

"Good evening," he said and leaned forward to peck

her cheek.

Well, I give Patty some credit; her friend has good taste in clothes. Bruce wore a dark blue suit, white shirt, and red striped tie. Angie caught a subtle hint of sandalwood in his cologne. His broad shoulders and flat midsection reminded her of Mac. Despite his receding hairline, Bruce was reasonably handsome.

"Good evening," she replied with a soft smile.

"I'm so glad you could make it. I've been looking forward to this all week."

Angie believed him. Regardless of the dim light, his pupils dilated more with every second she was there. She'd worn a straight skirt and silk blouse to work that day, and just swapped out her shoes for higher heels, fluffed her hair, and freshened her makeup for their date.

She was proud of herself for her appearance lately. At her age, her metabolism had been slowing down. For too long, she'd denied it, but knew she had to stop burying her head in the sand. Working out at the nearby gym wasn't her idea of fun, but if she was gonna be out on the market . . .

The sommelier approached the table, dressed similarly to the host—black suit and bow tie with a crisp white shirt. Could it be because when she came here with Mac, she never paid attention to what the serving staff wore? "Evening, folks. Can I assist you in a selection of wine to complement your dinner?"

Bruce held the wine list in his hand, but hadn't opened

it. "What are feeling like today, Angie, something red or white?"

How many calories are in a glass of wine? She'd never bothered to think about it.

"I think I'll have seafood tonight, so maybe white." She couldn't decide if she sounded congenial or timid. She forced a deep breath.

She fiddled with her napkin. She hadn't been on a date in *years*.

The sommelier made some recommendations as he pointed to the wine list. Bruce ordered a bottle of something expensive-sounding. She and Mac really hadn't purchased expensive wines. Maybe for a special occasion. But generally she'd pick up a bottle or two from the grocery store and whatever she bought seemed to suit Mac just fine. That and beer.

Stop thinking about Mac.

"So, Patty tells me you do Public Relations for l'Amour."

"Yes. I've been there for about six years, and I love it." She gave him a genuine smile. "Patty hasn't told me much about you. What do you do, Bruce?"

"I work in finance, well, treasury really, for Mettman Holdings. I've been there for almost five years."

A waiter filled two glasses with ice water and walked away. Then the sommelier returned and, after Bruce's approval, poured them each a half-glass.

"To a wonderful evening." Bruce stretched his arm, raising his glass in her direction.

Angie clinked her glass with his and took a healthy sip. "Delicious."

They took the opportunity to peruse the menu. As with most high-end restaurants, the menu was short but rich in variety.

"What looks good?" Bruce asked from across the small rectangular table.

"I'm thinking about the Scallops Provencal." She hadn't made scallops in years. She had a recipe Mac loved—heavy on the butter and lemon. Yum. Maybe she should hunt for that soon, if only to make it for the boys.

"Hmm. I think I'll go with the salmon."

The waitress looked about mid-twenties with her brown hair pulled back, dressed in a black skirt, white button-down shirt, and a black vest with a red VR embroidered on the chest. "Good evening, folks. I'm Jessica. Would we like an appetizer to begin with?"

Bruce glanced up from his menu. "See anything interesting, Angie?"

Oh, geez. She rarely ordered an appetizer. Shouldn't she just order her meal?

Relax.

"Whatever you'd like," she said with a small smile.

He ordered the jumbo shrimp cocktail. They still hadn't ordered their entrees. She took a large sip of her wine.

"So, as I was saying, I do finance for Mettman. Some people don't know but one of the ways companies make money is buying and selling currency."

Angie raised a brow. "You do currency trading?" She definitely did not expect that from a technology company. Clearly, she'd underestimated many behind-the-scenes functions of most companies.

"Well, that's part of it. The understanding of foreign exchange products and services is my main responsibility." He pitched forward in his chair slightly and pushed his shoulders back. "Just last month I was in Japan for a week investigating some investment opportunities in G10 currencies."

Bruce was obviously proud of his job, and although some of what he said went over her head, she could see Bruce was an intelligent man.

"Enough about me. Do you have any kids?"

"Yes, two teenage boys. One plays basketball, the other football."

"Nice. I bet you cart them all around then."

"Yes." She couldn't wait until Stuart got his driver's license, although then he'd want a car, and that just wasn't in the budget while in the middle of a . . .

"I have two boys myself and one girl. The boys are nineteen and seventeen, and Ella is twelve." The twinkle in his eye brightened when he spoke of his daughter. "She's so adorable when she Skypes me when I travel. I think it's mostly to make sure I bring her back a present," he said with a grin.

Mac believed in that, early on, bringing home gifts for her and the boys. She appreciated the surprise because he'd made an effort to think about what they each would like. That was something that had slowly trickled away.

Finally their appetizer arrived. Her lunch had worn off and she now felt distracted and on edge; hopefully the food would help.

She reached for a shrimp and dunked it in the cocktail sauce. "Mmm." Simply divine.

Bruce nodded. "These are exceptional."

"Are your boys interested in sports?" she asked between bites.

"Yes, Kyle likes soccer and Phillip likes baseball. Ella has also taken a liking to soccer, so things get pretty chaotic sometimes. My ex-wife and I have to coordinate our schedules too. I do the best I can when I'm in town."

Oh Lord. Another family-man who travels. She could feel the ex's pain.

Angie stared at the empty glass dish that held the shrimp. She squirmed in her seat, needing to eat. Needing to talk about something other than men who travel leaving their wives to carry the load.

When did you turn so cynical?

"Everything alright, Angie?"

"Maybe we should order." She softened her facial features to meet his gaze.

"Yes, of course." He scanned the restaurant for the waitress. "I'm getting hungry, too."

After they ordered, Bruce continued with a travel story. "This past summer I was in London. Wonderful city. I could not get over the sun rising at four forty-five in the morning."

Was that right? That's early.

His eyes rounded. "Surprising, right." He drank from his wineglass. "Have you ever been to London?"

"No. Although I'd love to go sometime." She savored another sip of wine and sat back in her chair.

"It's wonderful."

She got that. She bit her lip, holding back a laugh.

"First of all, it's nice that everyone speaks English as well. When you go, you must see a play." He gestured with his hand, palm up.

Just as she was about to ask what play he'd apparently gone to, he went full-steam ahead.

"I was able to catch *Phantom of the Opera,*" he said with a wave. "Such talent. However, you could see *Lion King* or *42nd Street* or *Les Miserables.*"

"Really?" She nodded, trying to act interested. She was at least thankful he wasn't talking about his work.

"Yes. And every play has its own theater. Genius. But anyway, in between my bank meetings and conference calls,

I had an excellent opportunity to see the city."

Yes, the wonderful city. She wiped her mouth with her napkin to stifle her giggle.

The waitress appeared, carrying food on her tray. It smelled so incredible, Angie's eyes tracked the plate of scallops placed before her.

Bruce smiled as he was served. "Thank you."

Jessica refilled their wineglasses. "Anything else I can get you both?"

Oh yes. Keep that wine coming. "No, thank you."

Jessica left and before Angie could take a bite, Bruce spoke. "Angie, the evening has barely started and I am having a wonderful time. You are so easy to talk to," he said, his eyes crinkling at the corners.

Angie smiled and tilted her head. She made the determination right then and there that Bruce's favorite word was *wonderful.*

To prevent the wine from putting impolite words in her mouth, she shoved in a bite of scallop. "Mmm."

They both ate in silence for several beats. Angie savored the silence *and* the mouth-watering dish.

After mere moments, Bruce began the conversation again.

A mild headache came on. Could it be the wine?

He spoke about his job—something about being predictive based on economic and political environments and their effect on the value of currency. Then, he filled her in on his and Kirstin's divorce, and how he didn't know what went wrong. He'd ask a question now and again, but never gave Angie much time to expand.

Bruce could talk more than anyone she knew. Possibly more than anyone on the planet.

Don't be mean.

When Jessica asked about dessert, Angie didn't hesitate. "No, thank you though." Facing her date, she said, "I really should be going."

"Oh, but it's only . . ." he glanced at his watch, "ten-fifteen." His tone pitched higher, confirming his surprise. "We'll take the check," he spoke to Jessica. "Wow, Angie I had no idea. The time has simply flown by."

"Mmm," she said with a closed-mouth smile. *Time flies when you do all the talking.*

Bruce paid the bill, and walked her to her car in the parking lot at the side of the building. "Angie, I had a wonderful time. I'd really love to see you again."

Oh boy. "Bruce, let's play it by ear. You and Kirstin have been divorced three years now. It's all still very new to me. Let's just give it some time."

Her answer seemed to appease him. He placed his hand on her arm and leaned in to kiss her.

She quickly presented her cheek. "Thank you for a wonderful evening, Bruce." *Oh no, it's contagious!*

"Thank you, Angie. I'll talk to you soon." He stepped back, and as she unlocked her car, he opened the door for her, wearing a hopeful smile.

She gave him a wave after he closed the door, and let out a long, bored sigh. It took all her energy not to slump in her seat as she was certain Bruce still had eyes on her.

Jesus, Marion, Joseph.

She drove as fast as legally allowed home. She wanted to kick off her heels, strip out of the clothes she'd been in all day, and climb into bed.

She replayed the date over in my mind. Bored was a good descriptor; Bruce's personality didn't quite mesh with hers. But she'd compared Bruce to Mac, more than once. Could that be the real reason she wanted the interminable date to end? Bruce wasn't Mac. She didn't know, but she *definitely* needed more time before diving into this whole dating scene.

Chapter
Fourteen

"T hanks, Louise," Mac said, leaning down to the open car window to speak to a mother of one of Stuart's teammates. Mac and Angie had known the Duff family for years, since Stuart and Ian had been in kindergarten together. Being Wednesday, Mac had his time with the boys at his apartment. Plus every other weekend, and alternating major holidays.

What a bunch of crap! Soon all of this would be ancient history; he was formulating a plan. The occasional text and compliment he'd pay Angie was just a start.

"You're welcome," she called out of the car window.

Stuart slung his gear bag over his shoulder and waved to his friend.

Mac appreciated the carpooling, and also appreciated Louise not saying anything about his and Angie's separation. Talking about it gave him a knot in his stomach.

Bags of Chinese take-out in his hands, Mac kicked the apartment door closed behind him. "Robbie, you here?"

"Yeah, Dad," Robbie called from the back bedroom.

"I have Chinese for dinner."

"I need a shower," Stuart called as he walked down the hall.

Mac was thankful for that. Teenage boy fresh from football practice did not make for an aromatic combination.

After Stuart had showered, they all sat at Mac's little kitchen table and ate. The boys devoured the food like they hadn't eaten in a month.

"How's school going?" he asked them both. Mac could see the grades online, but that only told part of the story. After a month of separation from their mother, he noticed the dip in grades, but knew they were refocusing their energies.

"Fine." Robbie scooped another bite of chicken fried rice.

Stuart looked up from his plate. "I need to go in early tomorrow to see my geometry teacher."

"Okay, we can do that." Then Mac remembered the most important thing going on in his son's life right now. "You got your learners' permit, right?"

"Yup," Stuart beamed before shoveling in another bite of sweet and sour chicken. "Came in the mail last Thursday."

"Well, we don't have time tonight, but this weekend, when you guys are over, we can go driving."

Stuart focused on Mac, eyes wide. "That would be great. I haven't had much driving time yet with Mom."

Mac resisted letting his disappointment show. Was

Angie mad at him and taking it out on the boys? "Why not?"

Robbie looked up and glanced at Stuart.

What are they not telling me?

"Well, she did take me out some this past weekend."

"Okay. Did you get to go out after school? Any nighttime driving?"

"Not really. She had an appointment one day and a kinda date another night."

Mac paused mid-bite.

A date! What the hell? They'd only been separated a month. What the fucking hell? Heat crawled up the back of his neck.

Calm down, Mac, have you forgotten about your date?

"Stuart," Robbie hissed.

Stuart glared at Robbie, then turned to face Mac. "Dad, she said she had a meeting, but told us later that she'd had a date. She wanted to be honest with us, she said. Someone had fixed her up."

What the hell could he say? He had to keep it together for the boys' sake. "Okay, it's alright, guys. Did you see him? What's his name?"

They both shook their heads. "She met him at a restaurant," Robbie offered.

What else happened? He had to stop the questioning. He couldn't pull the boys into the bullshit between him and his wife.

"I appreciate you sharing. Let's plan on going out this

weekend, Stuart, and logging some driving hours. Sound good?"

"Yeah. That'd be great."

They finished dinner and the boys did homework while he cleaned up the kitchen and tossed in a load of laundry. And the whole time, he fumed.

Someone had taken *his* wife out. He couldn't lose his cool. Again, he was no angel. He'd screwed up once and had to live with that for the rest of his life.

That didn't change the fact that he loved his wife. Hearing this news stung like a bitch, and there wasn't one thing he could do about it. The fact of the matter was the more time they spent apart, the harder it would be to get back together. Impossible, even, if Angie had been dating someone else.

Sonuvabitch!

CHAPTER
FIFTEEN

A ngie fumed. This must have been what Terri referred to as *getting ugly*. How dare Mac think he could keep the boys all summer, every summer. That news had been relayed to her that morning by her attorney. And Angie would *not* go back through her divorce lawyer. Oh no. She would handle this one directly.

She stomped off the elevator, her steps determined and sure. She debated blowing past his admin, but opted for professionalism instead. "Mimi, is my husband available?"

"Hi, Mrs. MacKey. Hang on. I'll check." The bubbly thirty-something woman picked up the phone and buzzed Mac.

Angie worked her jaw to unclench her teeth.

"He said to go right in."

Angie strode around Mimi's cubicle and pushed open the thick wooden door. She'd been to his new office only one other time, right after his promotion. The bookshelves were stacked with books, sales awards, a few momentos, and few pictures of her and the boys.

"Hey, Angie. What's up?" Mac said casually as he stood and rounded his impressive mahogany desk.

She closed the door behind her. Her eyes narrowed. "You know what's up, Mac," she uttered in a stern voice, deeper than she'd intended.

"Oh, is this about having the boys for the summer?"

He damn-well knew what this was about. He was toying with her. "Of course, it is. Why the hell else would I bother to come all the way downtown?" Her tone escalated.

He took three steps closer to her. She knew it was meant to intimidate, but she didn't move a muscle. "Look," he said, "you get the boys most of the time anyway. Now you can have your summers free."

Oh sure. He was thinking of her. *Not freakin' likely.* "You travel all the time." *Well, used to.* "How exactly is this beneficial for the boys? You think they'll enjoy just sitting around in your apartment all summer?"

He scoffed. "They will not."

"Of course they will."

"Oh, don't act like such a bitch," he growled.

Before anyone even saw it coming, Angie raised her right hand and sent it flying across Mac's cheek. The sound of the slap reverberated through the whole office. His cheek instantly reddened.

Her hands flew up over her gaping mouth and her eyes widened. Never in their years together had she ever hit him. There had never been violence. She'd rarely hit the boys growing up either, choosing other forms of discipline instead.

"Oh, crap. I'm sorry, Mac. I didn't mean to do that," she said behind cupped hands. "Oh, my God. I'm so sorry."

He stared at her for what felt like an eternity. She could see the fire in his eyes. He took a step closer, and she stepped back. Her back was now almost touching the door.

"No, you're not," he said, his voice low and menacing.

"Yes, Mac. I . . . I lost my head. I didn't mean to slap you."

"Prove it."

Confused, her eyebrows pinched together. "What? What do you mean? How?"

He reached beside her and locked his office door. "Prove it," he said again, but his voice sounded more hoarse and . . . lustful than before. He kept his eyes trained on hers.

She licked her lips and squirmed ever so slightly.

She didn't ask again, and Mac didn't wait. He simply pointed to his desk, the other hand on his hip, looking authoritative. Sexy and masculine. "Hands on my desk."

Angie had never seen this side of her husband before. Perhaps she should be scared, but in fact, his dominance only fueled her from the inside out. Her nether parts came alive. She wasn't exactly sure what he had planned, although she had a reasonably good idea. "What?" she sounded like a timid mouse, her question a bit too breathy.

Without giving her any more time to stall, he wrapped

his muscular arm around her waist and hauled her up against his body. His very rock hard body. *Oh my!*

"I said, put your hands on my desk. I'm going to spank that delicious ass of yours and *that* will show me just how sorry you are for slapping me," he spoke against her cheek. His warm breath sent a shudder through her. She shouldn't like this so much.

Then he let her go. Surprisingly, she maintained her balance. To do or not to do? She eyed him, then the desk. She bit her lip, and without any conscious thought, her legs moved, carrying her to the desk on their own volition.

Mac moved close behind. She stopped. He gently pushed against her mid-back, and bending at her waist, she placed her hands flat on his desk. He stepped closer to her, his erection digging into her hip. He whispered in her ear, "Look at this very fine ass leaning over my desk."

Words escaped her. Her brain could not function at a level high enough for her to mutter anything. He caressed a big, warm hand over her ass. Circling and circling. Then he pulled back and let his hand fly.

She tried to cry out, but the fear of being heard stopped her, so she squealed through her closed mouth. He did it again, smoothing her ass afterward. The sensation was inexplicable. It was at that very fine point where pleasure and pain met and the lines blurred. She panted.

Then she felt his hands reach for the hem of her straight skirt and shimmy it up her thighs and over her ass.

She wore a thong and her globes were now exposed. The position made her feel vulnerable, but insanely hot at the same time.

"I have always loved your lingerie," he breathed into her ear. She was a believer that just because you needed to be professional on the outside, didn't mean you couldn't be sexy underneath. Before she could thank him, *slap!* His hand came down over her bare ass hard. She shrieked louder before she could muffle it in her shoulder. This time his massages circled over her swollen achy nether lips. She knew he probably felt the dampness of her panties. She most certainly did.

Slap! The contact was lower although not as fierce. She moaned and let her head fall forward. Oh God, how much more of this could she take? Her ass was on fire, but her pussy ached for contact. She needed relief from Mac's hand.

"I see that these lovely things are getting wet. I think we should take them off." And he did just that. With deft fingers, he grabbed her panties on the right and left, and slowly dragged them down her legs. She stepped out of them without him uttering a word.

He stood. "Better," then *slap!* Direct contact over her aching pussy.

She moaned, and panted to damn-near hyperventilation.

"Do you need some relief, my sweet?" Even as he asked his long fingers gently, slowly played with her sex.

"Oh God."

He massaged her slickness around her lips and grazed over her clit. She moved her legs wider and pushed back into his hand.

Slap!

"Do you need me to fuck you, Angie?" he asked as the tip of his index finger pushed into her opening, twirling so slowly.

Oh, how she needed more. His finger was just a tease. She needed much more. "Yes," she gasped. "Please, Mac. Please fuck me."

He removed his finger, and immediately she heard the rasp of his zipper. Then she felt the head of his shaft stroke up and down her needy sex, spreading her juices more. He stopped and slowly pushed only the head inside her, no farther.

"Is this enough fucking for you, my sweet?" Thankfully he didn't wait for an answer. He drove all the way in. "Or do you need this?"

Her pussy clenched. "Yes," she breathed. "Yes, I need that."

He took a hold of her hips and began to pull back, almost completely out, and then pushed back in. His movements weren't fast. In a few brief moments, as if he couldn't maintain his own control, he pumped faster. She heard his breathing in time with hers. She began to push against him. They both moaned and built an incredible rhythm.

She was so close. "Oh, . . . don't stop, Mac," she panted.

That seemed to fuel him even more. The speed and pressure increased, and she was lost. Her hands bunched into balls, crinkling the papers beneath. A fierce orgasm streaked through her body, and recognizing its power, she turned her head in time to cry out in her shoulder, muffling most of the sound. Through it all, she heard Mac's grunt and knew he'd climaxed as well when his hands fell down alongside her on the desk. She heard his heavy breathing and felt his heaving chest against her back.

"Stay right there," he said in a low tone. He straightened, but didn't pull out. He reached into his pocket, and she felt the soft cotton handkerchief at her sex. He pulled out and wiped her a few times, collecting all the semen he could. Then he wiped himself, and put himself back together.

Angie stood and lowered her skirt back into place, then spun around to face him. For a few brief moments they stared at each other, wrapping their brains around what had just transpired. Mac dropped the handkerchief and stepped flush against Angie. He grabbed her face with both hands and crashed his lips to hers. Her tongue reached for his. She wrapped her arms around his neck and savored the feel of Mac's lips against hers, so firm, and soft at the same time.

All too quickly, he pulled back and released her head. "Perhaps I was a bit too hasty. I'll come up with another plan for the summers and get back to you." The corner of his mouth curved slightly, then he moved to the door to unlock it and pull it open.

That would be a predictable Mac-move—*we're done here, it's time to move on*. Never mind he was deep inside her not four minutes before. She smiled to herself, reached down to retrieve her panties, and slipped them into her purse. She walked over and placed her hand on the door handle.

"Yes, I would appreciate that. Something more agreeable for both of us." She pursed her lips, and she pulled the door open wider. "Have a nice day, Mac."

She sauntered to the elevator, not daring to look at Mimi. Lord only knew what the woman heard or thought was going on behind those walls. Angie might not return to Mac's office again until he had a new admin.

Geez, that was hot! She turned as the elevator doors closed, and was surprised to see Mac still standing there. Watching her.

Having sex on his desk had to be one of the fucking hottest things Mac had done in his entire life. And it was with his *wife*, no less. *Un-fucking-believable.*

He knew the exact moment the switch had been thrown, when Angie'd slapped him. Although he'd started it with the name-calling. He'd never called her names like that before, and he'd regretted it the second it came out of his mouth. But she'd slapped him before he had the chance to apologize. Something had snapped inside when she threw that slap. It stung, and in a hot-second an image of his hand connecting with her ass had flashed in his head.

What a dichotomy. She felt embarrassed and he grew hard.

Although it may have been an accident, he knew he was to blame for the whole episode. He'd had a bit of the devil in him when he'd told his lawyer to tell her lawyer he wanted the kids all summer. His lawyer thought him unreasonable, but probably didn't care too much since he was still racking up billable hours. Regardless, the tactic was all a ploy to get her to come to him. To his office. Deep inside, he still stewed over the fact she was dating. What bull!

I doubt she's thinking about another man now.

Her ass was spectacular and her pussy delicious. He knew just what to do to make her come. He may have gotten unimaginative and fallen into the traps of routine over the years, but he knew his wife's body better than some asshole.

He took in a deep breath and returned to his desk.

After that little encounter he knew he needed to have her gone, out, before he did anything more he might regret. He was the CMO for Chrissake, and these were business hours! He *could not* continue carrying on like that.

But damn if the images in his head didn't get him hard again as he resumed his work.

Angie strolled into the office a new woman. What had happened the day before at Mac's office was insanely hot. She licked her lips and took a deep breath. She'd slept like a baby and had dreamed of Mac. The feelings and thoughts that preoccupied her made it hard for her to focus and at the same time made everything so very clear.

"Oh," Nicole appeared at her cubicle, "I didn't hear you come in." Her head dropped to the side. "What happened to you?" she spoke slowly, as if analyzing and asking at the same time.

Angie raised her head and pushed her shoulders back. "Good morning. What's on the agenda today?"

"Uh-uh. You don't get to change the subject. What happened? You look relaxed. Really relaxed." Her eyes twinkled at Angie, and a smile pulled at her lips.

Angie rose from her chair and glanced down the aisle. "I can't talk about it now. I'm expecting Jarmon any second. Let's do lunch, okay?"

Nicole crossed her arms and tapped her foot—typical fun, sassy, comfortable-in-her-own-skin Nicci. "Fine. But this better be worth the wait."

Oh, it will be. She felt certain Nicci would do standing backflips after hearing her news.

"Angelique," Pierre Jarmon called from several feet away, "have you seen this article?"

Pierre had to be the most interesting boss Angie had

ever worked for. In some respects, very much the company president, but very personable and approachable when warranted—all fitting for a creative man that loved to live his life out loud.

He held up the morning edition of the Wall Street Journal. She'd seen it and knew he would stop by her office. Or cubicle. Whatever. "I have seen it," she said, watching his mouth move into a full-blown smile.

He took a breath and looked up at Angie. In her heels, she was taller than him. And having taller women around didn't seem to bother him in the least. He would always say, in the matter-of-fact way he had, *Hire women. They are brilliant.* "This is *magnifique.* They love the concept. They love the idea of the men's line at l'Amour."

"I knew they would." She smiled back at her boss.

He read from the paper. "L'Amour Lux dipped its toe in the menswear pond and turned it to gold. With brilliant, albeit little-known, designers making their appearance on the American fashion stage with l'Amour, the combination is a surefire formula for success. The clothing is quality, stylish, and leading the trend. Dare we expect anything less? L'Amour President Pierre Jarmon assures WSJ that after the completion of the market test in several US stores, the company will do a full rollout of the men's line to every store by the close of next year."

He gazed up. "You helped make this possible." He leaned in to wrap his arms around her and give her a big hug. "Thank you. *Merci,* Angelique."

Angie's eyes went wide in astonishment. When Pierre was in a good mood, everyone knew it. She chuckled and returned the hug.

"You're welcome." She'd just been doing her job.

"Oh, I need to tell Thomas now. *Au revoir.*" He flapped his hand and was gone in a flash.

Angie heard Nicole laughing from the other side of the cubicle wall. A laugh bubbled up in Angie as well.

Shortly after noon, Nicole appeared at her cubicle entryway. "Ready?"

Lunches with Nicci were quickly becoming ritual. Angie looked forward to this lunch hour in particular.

Angie and Nicci were seated at a little table in the corner.

"Okay, spill. This is more than great massage glow." Nicci paused with a twinkle in her eye. "Unless it was a very *special* massage," she said in a slow cadence.

Angie swatted at her arm. "No. Hush."

"You had sex," Nicole cut in.

She smiled, recalling the amazing sex she'd had on Mac's desk. "Yeah," she confessed in a low tone.

"I knew it. Who was it with? I thought you didn't like that guy Patty set you up with." Nicole glanced to the side. "What was his name?"

"Bruce."

"Right. Bruce. Was it him?" She wrinkled her nose at Angie.

Angie smoothed her lipstick. "No. It was Mac."

"What?!"

"Shh. Nicci." Angie gritted her teeth and quickly glanced around the restaurant.

"I'm sorry. I'm just so surprised."

"I know. Me too. It was an accident."

Nicole straightened in her chair and narrowed her eyes. "How do you accidentally have sex?" she asked in a lower volume.

"Well, . . . I slapped him."

Nicole's eyes rounded.

"He called me a bitch, so I slapped him."

"Good for you," Nicole praised her, but at the same time her brows pinched together.

Angie lifted her hand, palm out. "I know, but I really don't think he meant to . . ." she trailed off. Thoughts flooded her mind.

"What? I see those wheels turning. You don't think Mac meant to call you a bitch?"

"No," she started slowly. "I mean yes. I don't know, Nicci. Thinking back, I'm wondering if the whole incident was planned."

"How do you mean?" Nicci took a sip of her iced tea and leaned forward.

"Through our lawyers, Mac said he wanted the boys

with him during the summer. The whole summer."

"That's outrageous."

"I know. So I went to his office to confront him, but being selfish like that doesn't sound like Mac. Does it?" She asked more for her own benefit than Nicci's.

"No, but he has been trying to reach out to you more." Nicci lifted her fork for a bite.

Angie rested her elbow on the table and chewed at her thumbnail. "I think that was all a ploy to get me to confront him." She shook her head, realizing just how absurd that reasoning sounded. "I don't know, Nicci. I think my imagination is getting the best of me."

Nicci shrugged, and they both took bites of their salads.

"Unless, . . ." Nicole started. "What if it *was* a calculated move?"

"But why? Just to make me mad? We've had years of that crap."

"You know how the boy in school will be mean to the girl he likes?"

Angie tipped her head. "This isn't grade school. We're both grown adults, or supposed to be." She definitely saw that Mac had goaded her.

"What I'm saying Angie is, what if he's trying to get you back?"

What? Could Nicci be right? "I don't know." It seemed like a plausible explanation. And that sex was hot. If she could have it that hot again—many times again—she'd get back together with him.

Oh God, did she really just think that? After everything they'd been through, could she really go back into that marriage? If it were different, perhaps. She still loved Mac, however all the crap got in the way of those deep feelings. Maybe he was thinking the same thing.

Nicole let her think in quiet for several moments, then she spoke. "The question is really, what do you think? And what do you want the answer to be?"

Angie raised the speed on the gym's treadmill. Lately, she found jogging was great for helping her to think. Maybe it was improved blood flow, getting oxygen to the brain. Who knew? But she admired the results just the same—her clothes were fitting better too. She hadn't worked out in years, and shame on her. Energetic activity did her body good. Even her mood brightened.

Angie replayed her conversation with Nicci from lunch. She was becoming obsessed over whether or not to try and get back together with Mac. Did *he* even want to? What if Nicci was completely wrong? What if he'd been overtaken by a surge of testosterone causing him to have sex with her in his office and he really had no interest in getting back with her?

Geez! The boys were at his place for the weekend, until Sunday at six. That meant no distraction—she had all weekend to mull this over. And over.

CHAPTER
SIXTEEN

A ngie popped the lid off her lip liner, and very carefully lined her lips. God, she never wore lip liner. Then she filled in the area with a luscious red. Nothing too bright nor one that screamed harlot. A just-the-right-red.

Earlier that Monday morning, Stuart had bustled around the kitchen asking if anyone had seen his science book. Of course, no one had, so that ratcheted up his stress level.

"Did you leave it at your father's?" Angie had asked him.

"I must've." Stuart retrieved his cell phone from his back pocket and called his father to ask him to drop it off after work. The tone in Stuart's response made Angie believe that Mac had begrudgingly agreed.

Since that very moment, Angie had been scheming. If anybody had seen her face, the twinkle in her eye and the grin across her lips would be obvious.

Angie had managed to break away during her lunch hour for a mani-pedi. The helpful girl at the salon had told her where to find a matching red lipstick. Standing in front of her bathroom mirror, she smoothed her lips together, then slid on her new black pumps that fit her like a glove—designer and worth every penny. She stood back from her full-length mirror and checked out the woman in the reflection. Black dress, silky black hose, black peep-toe heels, and dangling silver earrings.

Stunning. Probably an eight out of ten. Angie smoothed her hands over her waist and hips. The woman in the mirror smiled.

The doorbell rang.

Showtime.

"Mom! Dad's here," Robbie called from the kitchen.

"Okay, I'll get it." Heaven forbid he get up and answer the door when he knew it wasn't for him. She grinned inside that her sons were so predictable.

She took a deep breath, pushed her shoulders back, and opened the front door.

"Hey, I've got—" Mac stopped himself. She held back a smile as she witnessed Mac's eyes go wide and his jaw lax.

"Hi, Mac."

His gaze traveled the length of her. It had been a long time since he'd looked at her that way. The way you look at something you want to devour entirely with no apologies. Her heart jumped a beat.

He wore a dark charcoal suit, and his tie hung loosely from a long day at the office.

"Hey, Angie. I've got . . . I mean . . . wow. You look great."

Ah, just the reaction she was looking for—compliments plus lack of proper diction meant indelible impression. The kind of impression that hopefully got him thinking about her well into the night. No matter who else he was with, she wanted Mac thinking about her. And only her.

"Thanks."

"Got a date?" The flash of bitterness in his eyes was quick, but she caught it.

She merely smiled a knowing smile and opened the door wider for him to enter. He walked through but still didn't take his eyes off her.

"Stuart, your father's here with your science book," she called upstairs.

Stuart yelled back, "Coming."

And sure enough, she heard the pounding of his size eleven shoes as he raced down the stairs and to the foyer. "Thanks, Dad."

"You're welcome. Next time, make a pass before you go to make sure you haven't forgotten anything. Okay?"

"Yeah, I will." Stuart raced back upstairs, book in hand.

"Well," she stood watching, waiting and, of course, smiling. A smile that had just the right amount of teeth showing. She didn't want to appear like she was trying too hard.

"Well, . . . I guess I better head out."

"Sure, okay."

He turned toward the door. "Have a good time tonight."

"Thanks. I will." That sounded casual enough.

As he stepped onto the front porch, he turned one last time to get a look at her. He grinned and then spun back around and headed for his German car parked in the driveway. A quality car built to last. Mac would always tell the boys, *Take care of your stuff and it will last forever.*

She closed and locked the front door. A huge smile grew across her face. *Mission accomplished.*

"How do you guys feel about pizza for dinner?" she called out.

"Great," she heard in unison.

She called and ordered an extra-large with everything on it, then went to her closet to hang up her dress, and slip on some sweats and a tee.

Mac admittedly had felt annoyed when Stuart asked him to bring the science book he'd forgotten at the apartment over the weekend. Mac had hoped to get to the gym that night. Then he remembered the kid was reasonably responsible and this probably wasn't going to be a reoccurring thing. He would give Stuart the benefit of the doubt. Of course, any bit of irritation quickly dissolved when Angie opened the door. Holy fuck! She looked fucking amazing.

The fruits of her working out were apparent in that black dress she wore—the way it cinched at her waist, and hugged her hips and breasts. Her face looked bright and happy. Her hair shinier than he'd remembered, and longer. And those legs of hers appeared to be a mile long in those damn high-heels.

Holy fuck!

She had a fucking date. Again! The divorce hadn't even been finalized and she was dating. *Well, duh. So did you—sort of.* He shook his head. He didn't want to think about that.

Mac plodded into his empty apartment, dropped his keys on the counter and proceeded to his bedroom. He started to get out of his suit, his escalated breathing the only sound in the room. He whipped off his tie and threw it on the bed. Then he sat in a chair, and removed his shoe so fast it went flying, slamming into the wall with a *whap!*

Alright, calm down, Mac.

He couldn't stop thinking about how Angie looked standing before him. She was smoking hot, and some loser was taking her out tonight. *His* wife, goddammit!

Okay, so he might not be putting on a full-court press at this point, but he couldn't risk scaring her away. Regardless, this wasn't right. Nowhere near close to being right!

Mac followed Stuart into the apartment and dropped his backpack and football bag on the floor. Robbie sat at the kitchen table reading a textbook.

"Hey, Robbie."

"Hey, Dad."

Mac rolled up his sleeves and began pulling food and a beer out of the refrigerator. Wednesday night was his night with the boys.

He tried to work quietly so he wouldn't disrupt Robbie's concentration. Just then his phone dinged with a new text. Ryan.

Bro, you free next week for dinner? Steaks on the grill.

Mac grinned as he pulled up his calendar.

Can't say no to steaks. Tuesday or Thursday are best for me. Thanks.

Ryan replied quickly. *Great. Tuesday it is.*

Time spent with friends helped keep Mac's sanity through all this. He couldn't wait.

Mac dropped the brats on the stovetop grill, a perfect dish for a cold October evening, when his mind went to Angie. He didn't know how to broach the topic with his boys of her date. He had replayed that night seeing Angie a million times since Monday evening. She seemed different. She looked great. Had she always looked that good and he'd missed it?

He'd gotten the impression her date from weeks ago

had amounted to nothing. He could tell though, this time was different. Was it, in fact, getting serious, or had she met someone else?

"Okay, guys, clear the table. Dinner's ready."

Mac watched as the boys dug into their food. He remembered those years when he could eat fast and often. There'd been times growing up he felt hungry constantly.

"So, how's the week going?"

"Good," they both mumbled with full mouths.

"Robbie, have you started basketball practice?"

"Yeah. Our first game isn't for a few weeks. Did Mom send you our schedule?" He looked up.

"Yes, I think I saw it on my email. It's a home game."

"Uh-huh."

Now that the topic had been brought up . . . "How's your mother?"

"Fine," they both said.

"How did her date go Monday night?"

"What date?" Stuart asked.

"When I dropped off your science book, I thought she had a date."

Stuart looked over at Robbie, and they both frowned. "She didn't have a date. We ordered pizza and watched American Pickers."

"Dad, you should've seen it. Mike found this pre-World War II motorcycle in great condition. He tried talking the guy into letting him ride it and . . ." Robbie rattled on, but

Mac's mind wandered.

Angie *didn't* have a date that night.

He fell speechless. Why was she dressed up then? Come to think of it, she didn't *confirm* having a date, he thought. He'd assumed she had a date.

Well, fuck me.

Mac shoved a bite in his mouth to cover the smile on his face, and refocused on Robbie. His wife had dressed like that *for him*. To get his attention. Well, it had worked. They still had a chance. Now, how to reel her in and close the deal?

CHAPTER
SEVENTEEN

"**H**ey, man. You made it." Ryan opened the front door of his contemporary-style house, a twenty-minute drive from Mac's house, in a newer neighborhood. "C'mon back. Carol's got the kids at some school function, so we have some peace and quiet before they get home."

Ryan's kids were nine and seven, and balls of energy. He remembered that age with Stuart and Robbie. They had two speeds—fast and sleep.

Mac chuckled. "Your kids are great."

He followed his friend through the house to the back covered patio. The temperature had dropped recently—just right for chilling outside. Ryan reached into a cooler and pulled out an ice-cold beer, handing it to him.

"Thanks."

"So, how's living on your own?" Ryan kept his sight trained on Mac as he asked the question.

Mac exhaled, and shrugged a shoulder. "I'm surviving. There's been some adjusting. It's been a weird few weeks."

"How so?" Ryan flipped the steaks and checked the

foil-wrapped potatoes.

"I'll start with the bad news." That got Ryan's attention and he turned toward Mac with a frown.

"You mean, besides moving out?"

"Yes." He scratched the side of temple. "After we met at Borrowed Money for drinks, a woman approached me. She had one thing on her mind."

Ryan sat in the chair across from him at the glass and black wrought iron dining table. He raised an eyebrow, clear about Mac's reference.

"I told her I wasn't interested. She seemed to accept that, and asked if I could walk her to her car. She put on a full-court press." Mac shook his head, still in complete disgust with himself, and his deplorable lack of willpower.

"Anyway, it almost went too far before I caught myself. Frankly, I'm sick about it and I think I need to tell Angie."

Ryan shook his head at once. "Fuck no. Don't tell her."

Mac raised his eyes and saw the earnestness in Ryan's gaze.

"It happened one time, right?"

Mac nodded.

"And this was after several drinks, right?"

"That doesn't matter, Ryan."

"In a way it does. Mac, the bottom line is you can't tell Angie to relieve *your* guilt. You screwed up. It won't happen again. You need to deal with it on your own and move past this. You want to get Angie back, right?"

The man had a valid point. He would be relieving his own guilt and in the process tearing up Angie. She would be mortified, and she might never forgive him. He'd never cheated before and that woman got him at a low-point in his life. That was *never* going to happen again. Still, honesty was the best policy. "Of course, I do. But—"

"No buts. Focus on Angie and moving forward. Have you seen her?"

The corner of Mac's lip quirked up. "Yes. Funny you should ask."

Ryan's demeanor relaxed. "I'm listening."

"She came down to my office to ream me out about something I did." He wasn't about to get into the details of how he'd intentionally taunted his wife. "Well, one thing lead to another, and in the heat of the moment, I took her. On my desk."

"Hell no," Ryan said stringing out the words with a gleam in his eyes. "How was it?"

"Fuckin' crazy good. Like it hadn't been that good in *years*."

"So what did you do? Call her for a date? What?" He heard the hope in Ryan's voice.

"No." Frankly, he was paralyzed with fear that he'd screw something up, and lose his chance at getting her back.

"*No!* Why not?" Ryan leaned forward in his chair.

"I guess I just considered it a slip. An accident." He scratched the back of his head. "I need to figure out my next move."

"And this was like two weeks ago? Bro—"

Mac held up a hand before Ryan tore into him. "Wait. There's more."

Ryan exhaled. "Okay, let's hear it." He sat back and rested his hands on the arms of the chair.

"Stuart forgot a book at my place and I drove by the house last Monday night after work to drop it off. Angie looked like a million bucks, like she was dressed for a date."

"A date on a Monday night. It could happen," Ryan said as he teetered his chair back and forth.

"But that's just it. There was no date. When I had the boys Wednesday night, they said they'd stayed in, ate pizza, and watched TV."

Ryan narrowed his eyes. "No date, but she was dressed up."

"Right," Mac said taking a swig of his beer.

"You know what that means, right?" Ryan rose to tend the grill.

"That she might want me back."

"Bingo," he said pointing the tongs directly at Mac. "So what's your plan?"

"I don't know. I've been thinking about it all week."

Ryan returned to his seat and drank the last of his beer. "You gotta find a way to woo her. Like write her a love letter."

Mac nearly gagged at the thought. "That's not really

me, Ry."

"I don't give a shit. Girls like that stuff. And you can't do what you normally would have done, because clearly that shit didn't work," he said poignantly.

Mac sighed and nodded in resignation. "You're right. I need to come up with something new. Something unexpected."

"Exactly."

Before the conversation could continue, Ryan's kids, Marissa and Billy, ran through the house and to the back patio. "Uncle Mac," they yelled in unison as they clobbered him for hugs.

"Hey, guys. How's it going?"

"Great." The kids had rosy cheeks like they'd been exercising or something. Marissa had her hair in pigtails and wore pink from her head to her toes. Billy was a foot shorter and the spitting image of his father, with lighter hair.

Carol strolled out through the sliding glass doorway. "Hey, Mac. Glad you're here. It's good to see you."

Mac stood to hug his friend. "Nice to see you too. You're looking well, Carol."

"Thanks." She smiled.

"Kids, go wash up. Dinner's ready," Ryan announced.

"Okay, Daddy," Marissa said, and she and her brother ran inside.

Carol went to her husband and placed a kiss on his lips.

"Hey. I'll go get dishes and silverware. Be right back."

The five of them sat on the back patio, eating, enjoying the food, the conversation, and the temperature. Talking with Ryan about his guilt helped alleviate the knot in his stomach somewhat.

At the end of the great evening, Mac helped with the clean up and said his thank yous and goodbyes.

"Keep me posted on developments," Ryan said referring to his situation with Angie.

"I will. Thanks again, man." Mac drove away feeling full, and having a motivation toward his marriage he hadn't felt in years.

The thought hit him like a truck. Staying motivated about his marriage was something he should have been doing all along. Shit! *This isn't rocket science.*

He knew Angie wanted him back, but clearly she was testing the waters. Testing him. He had one chance to win her back. He would *not* screw it up. The big question remained: how to seduce his wife?

CHAPTER
EIGHTEEN

T he package arrived at her office at ten Wednesday morning by courier. Angie studied the blue envelope, no return address. Her eyes narrowed. She hadn't been expecting anything. Is this something professional or personal, she thought as she slipped open the seal.

She slid out a simple white card with block lettering. She recognized the handwriting and her heart stopped.

I can't stop thinking about what happened in my office.
M

She gasped and quickly covered her mouth with her hand. She stared at the note. What did this mean? He was mad about the slap or—she swallowed hard—he was excited about the sex.

Seriously, Ang, you have to ask?

She bit down on her lip, trying not to smile. God, the sex they'd had was amazing. Stellar. Visions rushed back into her mind of how he'd looked, his penetrating eyes after she slapped him. The feel of his hand caressing her. The smell of him as he leaned in close to her. His amazing cock stroking her deep inside. She wanted that again. She wiggled in her chair. Faint wetness gathered at her sex from the mere thought of what had happened over two weeks ago.

He'd noticed her. That was it. When she dressed up last Monday. God, it worked.

Now what? What should she do?

She stuck the note back in the envelope and into her purse, and opened her email program when Jarmon stood near her and Nicci's cubicles.

"Ladies, I have good news."

They both swiveled around to face their boss.

"The offices on the fifth floor are almost complete. How do you both feel about moving in next week?"

Executives, department heads, and, of course, Jarmon, had their offices on the fifth floor, the highest floor of the building.

The women stood. "Wow, almost done," Nicci said as she glanced Angie's way.

"*Oui.*"

"Well, that's great," Angie replied, her stomach turning with mixed feelings.

"I will have Clarisse send the schedule over. I wanted to tell you myself. I am very much excited to have you close by once again."

Angie smiled at Jarmon's sincere comment. He was the best boss she'd ever had.

After he left, Nicci leaned on their adjoining wall. "I'm not sure how I feel about this. I mean, you've been right here for months. Now, I doubt our offices will be next to each other."

"I know. I was thinking the same thing."

"You know what? I'll take Clarisse out to lunch. See what she can do about placing us next to each other," Nicci said with a wink.

"Great idea."

Having Nicci close by, especially with all the chaos in her life, was a God-send. It might make her sound four instead of forty-four, but having her friend close was comforting. Angie would secretly cross her fingers. But whether their offices were next to each other or not, she would learn to adapt. Adapting was the motto of her life lately.

Now what? That was the million dollar question after Mac had the note delivered to Angie's office.

One theme resonated throughout Mac's entire being when he thought about how to salvage the relationship with his wife—make the sex amazing for her. The unconventional, erotic sex they'd had in his office told a very potent story.

He thought long and hard about the two of them. She

needed the kind of spontaneous, hot, audacious sex they'd had in their early years of dating. Sex wouldn't fix everything in their marriage, but he knew it would be a start.

So why hadn't she said something to him earlier? Told him what she needed?

He scratched his scalp and smoothed his hair. He recalled an article he'd read in a men's magazine years ago. *As a rule, women don't like to talk about sex*, he recalled. Mac hadn't understood it at the time, but slowly the idea became salient. Women will talk about sex in general, but when it relates to what they want in the bedroom, not a chance.

That put the ball in Mac's court to implement a fix.

He squinted his eyes and played their office escapade over in his head, for the billionth time. Mac had been uncharacteristically dominant and commanding toward Angie. His cock twitched at the thought. He liked it *and* so did she. She'd become slicker than he'd ever felt. God, she looked so good bent over his desk— her smooth, round ass ready for his touch.

Mac steepled his fingers together. Ideas were flying through his mind faster than floor trading on an old-fashioned stock exchange. He would make it good for her. If he played it right, it would be the first of many such nights with his wife.

Mimi buzzed his line. "Mac, Will Manning wants to know if you can meet with him and the manufacturer of the water recycler tomorrow afternoon at three."

He leaned forward in his chair and toggled to his calendar. "Sure, but I have a meeting with Camille at the same time."

"That's why I called you."

His admin was brilliant. That was definitely *not* a meeting he needed to be in. Hell, Camille didn't need to have the meeting. She could easily send her comptroller to review quarter-end and year-end sales projections.

"Thanks, Mimi. I'll take care of Camille. Please tell Will I'll be there." Getting the water recycler up and running was paramount at this point. He wouldn't miss that meeting for the world.

Then he picked up the phone and dialed his local district manager, Rhea.

"Hey, Mac."

"Hey, Rhea. Are you free tomorrow at three for a review of sales projections with Camille? I need to be at manufacturing."

He heard her typing. "Ah, yeah."

"Great. I'll shoot over the latest projections. It's everything we've gone over last week."

"Shouldn't be a problem."

"Thanks." He disconnected the line, and sent the spreadsheet. Camille may be surprised by Rhea's presence, but he had complete confidence in Rhea. Not to mention, some distance from Camille for a while might be a good thing.

The receptionist rang Angie's desk phone Thursday as she'd returned from lunch.

"Angie, you have a delivery here. Can you come get it?"

Her heart skipped a beat. *Mac.* "Sure. Be there in a sec," she replied. She licked her lips and willed herself to walk at a normal pace. Her heart rate sped. How was it that she became so excited over the husband she was supposed to be divorcing?

As she crossed the building toward the receptionist desk, tall red roses stood at attention, in a crystal vase with sprigs of greenery.

"Hey, Angie. These sure look pretty, and they smell good, too," the receptionist said with a twinkle in her eye.

"Thanks." Angie hefted the dozen roses, beyond eager to read the card.

She returned to her cubicle and several heads turned to admire her present. Including Nicci.

"Wow. What do you have there?" she asked.

Angie inhaled the fragrant roses and slipped the card from its stand. "A present," she said, not the least bit concerned about the smile plastered on her lips.

Meet me at the W lobby bar tomorrow at 7. I want to see that dress again.

M

That dress? Oh, yes. The dress she'd worn when he came to the house and thought she had a date. That dress hugged her like it was custom-made. L'Amour had the best designers. Her mouth curved. She loved that dress, the heels, the red lipstick—the whole ensemble.

"Mmm," escaped from her throat.

"Is it from Mac?"

She glanced up at Nicci, standing in her cube. "He wants to meet Friday— Wait! Friday! Stuart probably has a football game."

She tossed the card on her desk and quickly swiveled her chair around to bring up the game schedule online. A few clicks and . . . it was a bye week. She exhaled. Crisis averted.

"How's it look?"

"It's a bye."

"So what are you going to do?"

"Well, I'll meet him—" Was this something she truly wanted?

"Yes?" Nicci tipped her head, her eyebrows raised.

"Hell, I don't know, Nicci. Part of me wants to go, and the other says 'why bother'."

Nicci chuckled and leaned in close. "I know about the parts that want to go," she said with a benevolent smile.

"Nicci," Angie scolded her.

She wanted to go. Bottom line, the curiosity stirred her

in unexpected ways. She needed to know what he would do, what he had planned.

Oh, God, please tell me he has something amazing planned for us.

She frankly wasn't interested in the same-ol' sex. A woman had fantasies. She envisioned sex the way it was early in their marriage, when Mac had fulfilled those fantasies.

Angie slumped in the chair.

CHAPTER
NINETEEN

T he hotel bar was richly appointed in dark wood
paneling, hardwood floors, and a glossy, deep-
mahogany bar with amber bottles lining the glass shelves
behind it.

Mac stood back in a dark nook of the bar, watching his
wife sip on chardonnay.

Christ, she looked amazing. How was it he'd missed
how gorgeous she really was? Her smile brightened when
the barman refreshed her drink. His sight traveled the curve
of her jaw, the graceful descent to her neck to her jeweled
décolletage and inviting cleavage.

He imagined running his hands down the curvature of
her back as it led him to her perfectly rounded, heart-
shaped ass. His dick began to strain in his pants with the
images of Angie's naked body spread out before him.

It had been years since he had such vivid fantasies of
his wife. And if this would be their turning point, he would
battle every day to keep their sex life alive and not take her
for granted.

No truer words were spoken when Mac spied a sharp-dressed man, about six-three, wearing a charismatic white smile in a designer suit cross toward his wife. Angie loved designer suits. Likely because of her job with a high-end clothier. The stranger resembled Will Demps, only taller. He stepped right up to Angie and greeted her with confidence.

Mac witnessed Angie turn on her stool to meet his gaze, offering her own beautiful smile. He felt himself getting warm under his tie as the man held out his hand and shook hers. He then leaned forward and whispered something in her ear. As she laughed at his words and tossed her shiny brown hair, Mac wondered if she was being friendly or flirting. She hadn't worn her wedding ring, after all.

Mac was seconds from blowing a gasket when Angie finally shook her head at the man. His face fell in disappointment.

Damn straight. She's mine.

A waitress passed behind him, and Mac quickly caught her arm. "Excuse me. Would you kindly give this note to the woman at the bar in the black dress?" He pointed, then handed the waitress the envelope and a twenty.

She pocketed the twenty. "Sure."

Mac watched the waitress wend around the tables to Angie seated at the bar. She handed Angie the envelope, said a few words, and walked away.

The Demps look-a-like waited patiently—hovered really—as Angie opened and read the note. She smiled and glanced around the bar, as if searching for him.

She looked up at the stranger, said something, and shook his hand. As she rose on her heels, she flagged the barman for the check.

Perfect. She'd had a glass or two of wine, enough to loosen her mood, and she appeared to have no problem blowing off Mister Comehomewithme.

Mac slipped easily from the bar and strode to the bank of hotel elevators. He would wait again in the shadows for Angie before he set his plan into action.

Angie buzzed with anticipation as she waited for Mac at the bar. He apparently was running late because during that time a tall, dark, and handsome man approached her. He'd laid on some delightful compliments in a deliciously deep voice that brought Angie's nipples to a peak. The man flattered her and perhaps if she wasn't married, she'd entertain having dinner with him. Truthfully, since receiving Mac's flowers, he was all she could think about.

The bartender brought the check. Angie laid down some cash and grabbed her purse. She strolled to the elevators, managing her pace.

Mac's note read: *Meet me in my room on the 10th floor. You don't know me.*

He didn't give her a room number, but she had to

believe it would be evident which room was his once she arrived. The last part of his note sent a thrill through her. What was he up to?

She took several breaths as she waited, surrounded by a handful of businessmen and one woman. The doors parted and Angie walked in. She pressed the number ten for her floor, and her breath hitched as Mac strolled in shortly before the doors closed.

"Good evening." He flashed a smile and stood next to her, facing front.

She nodded. "Hello." But couldn't help her smile. He looked positively scrumptious. She loved seeing Mac in a suit—charcoal gray with a red silk tie, no less. Handsome as sin.

One man and the woman exited when the doors opened on the third floor. She saw Mac pivot her way and stare at her.

She turned her head to face him. "Yes?"

"Forgive me if I'm too forward, but how would you like to come back to my room for a drink?" he asked.

Conversation in the elevator ceased. Angie looked at the others and saw their stunned expressions. Her heartbeat ratcheted up another level.

She smiled flirtatiously, responding to the twinkle in his eyes. "I've been waiting all night for someone to ask me. I'd love to."

He smiled back at her and waited for the doors to open

on the tenth floor before saying, "After you."

He placed his warm hand on her lower back, guiding her into the hall. He stopped in front of his hotel room door and used the keycard. "Please, come in," he directed as he held the door open for her.

The room was more spacious than a typical hotel room. A large bed dressed in white with pale green accents was positioned against a large wall to the right. She noticed Mac's carry-on roller bag in the corner. Her gaze scanned the room and landed on the table in front of the floor-to-ceiling windows. There, rested a bottle of champagne in an ice bucket and a plate of cheese, sausages, bread, and fruit.

"You can leave your bag on the chair," Mac said as he casually walked to the table and poured two glasses of champagne. He handed one to her and clinked her glass.

"Cheers."

They both sipped the bubbly wine. It felt so good going down. Angie had an anxiousness inside, like she was on a job interview for a really great job with her potential, uber-masculine boss, and she didn't want to blow it.

He spoke first. "I'm Steven MacKey, but you can call me Mac." He offered his hand.

She took it and replied, "Angie. Good to meet you."

He held onto her hand and cocked his head. "Your parents named you Angie?"

She smiled. She had to admit—she loved this game. She gently shook her head. "Angelique. After my great grandmother. She was French."

He lifted her hand to his mouth. He ever so slowly kissed her knuckles while keeping his eyes trained on hers. "Angelique," he whispered.

Oh shit! She licked her lips, and felt the moisture begin to pool at the apex of her thighs.

He released her hand, and it was like the spell was broken. She breathed again.

"Care for a little something to eat?" He motioned to the plate. "I thought you might be hungry."

She reached for a bite of summer sausage, cheese, and bread. "Yes. Thank you. I haven't eaten since lunch."

His face stayed neutral, but his eyes blazed heat. "I watched you in the bar downstairs. I saw you drinking wine, but you had no food," he said casually.

Her lips parted. He'd watched her. She nodded slowly and bit into the cheese. Mac popped a piece of meat into his mouth, followed by a chunk of cheese.

"What else did you see?"

His nostrils flared. "Well, Angelique, I saw a handsome man hit on you. He looked very much like he wanted to take you home and fuck you."

Her breath audibly hitched. Those were words Mac rarely used, and it surprised her how much she liked hearing them. At least her body did. The ache in her nether region escalated.

He had a look to him that oozed power and control. A

side of him that in twenty years, Angie had *rarely* witnessed. Was this why he was so successful at work?

Angie decided on a nonchalant response. She reached for a piece of fruit, shrugged, and rounded the table to look out the window. "I suppose he did." She glanced over her shoulder at him, then turned back toward the window and the lights of downtown Dallas, with no real clue as to what she was viewing. Her mind couldn't keep up when her body had so many wonderful ideas of its own. She sipped on her champagne, refraining from gulping the entire contents down.

"I see," Mac said as he strode up behind her. "But you're here now."

"It would appear so," she nonchalantly agreed.

"And you know what that means?" He didn't wait for a response. He grabbed her hips, pulled her back, and pressed her into his growing arousal. "It means *I* get to fuck you," he whispered low in her ear.

A shiver ripped through her, and she may have moaned. She couldn't be sure because with a fistful of hair, he gave a little tug, pulling her head to the side, exposing her neck. He brought his mouth down to her sensitive skin and laid kisses on her throat. Warmth rocketed through her body. It wasn't supposed to feel this good. And yet, jubilation filled her to the core.

She shifted her legs closer together, pressing against the ache at her sex.

"Angelique, finish your wine and hand me the glass," he breathed behind her ear.

She did as she was told—handed him her glass, but didn't turn around. He set her glass on the table and returned his attention to her.

"I want to see the gorgeous body you have hiding under this dress. Tantalizing me," he spoke with a rasp in his voice as he slowly lowered her dress zipper down her back.

The compliments. God, how she loved to hear the compliments from Mac. Never before had she realized she wanted them—needed them—so much.

He slid the dress off her shoulders, but it couldn't go farther. It clung to her hips.

Mac's fingertips swept up her back in a teasing manner. The room fell silent, with only the sound of their breathing. She wondered what he was thinking. Maybe he recognized that she wore new lingerie. It would be her secret that this was the set she'd purchased online about eight years prior. Now he got to see it.

She prayed he would do something soon or else she might explode.

"This is a pretty black and red bra, Angelique. Makes me think of fire. Fire that I suspect you have deep inside you." His hands came across her torso, pulling her flush to his front, and making their way up to cup her breasts.

She let her head lull back against his shoulder.

He yanked the lace down over her breasts, and

instantly toyed and tugged at her nipples. The throbbing at her sex was excruciating now. If anyone could see them through the window, she had too much lust and passion coursing through her to give a damn. She was seeing a side of Mac she hadn't ever seen. And she *loved* it.

"I could take you like this, right now. Push you up against this window and take you from behind. Something tells me you'd like that," he said in her ear.

"Yes, please," she whimpered.

"Turn around. I'm taking off that sexy dress."

She pivoted on her heels to face him. He grabbed two handfuls of dress and commanded, "Down on your knees."

Her eyes widened briefly before she did as he bid. Bracing one hand on the glass, she lowered herself while Mac pulled the dress up and over her head. He threw it to a chair.

Mac then began to work his belt and pants zipper. He pushed down the fabric enough to free his erection. Her sight moved back and forth, from his eyes to his cock. He was so gloriously hard. Hard for her.

He wrapped a hand around his cock and stroked it several times. She licked her lips in anticipation.

"You have me so hot, I'm going to need some relief, Angelique. Do you think you're up for the task?"

"Yes," she breathed.

"Hands on my thighs and open that remarkable mouth of yours."

As she placed her hands flat on his legs for support, he cupped the back of her neck and brought her to within an inch of his cock. Using his fist, he glided the tip over her lipstick-red lips before feeding it all the way in.

He groaned.

Mac was dominating her; she was his submissive. They had never played these kinds of games before. Her panties were soaked by his words, his commands, his touch. She couldn't get enough.

She rewarded him with her mouth—taking him as far as she could and sucking on the way up.

After several strokes, he said, "Sweet Jesus. Woman, you are going to make me come." He pumped into her mouth several more times before he stopped.

She peered up at him, questioning. The residue of red lipstick coating him.

"That's all for now. Stand up and go lie down on the bed."

She rose and went to lay across the bed, wearing only a necklace, her bra, panties, and heels. Mac stripped, and laid his jacket and tie over the chair. He prowled closer, his gaze trained on her.

His physique was incredible for a forty-six year old man. Strength and muscle and power. He maintained his body, and she took her fill of the beautiful sight.

"I'm going to taste you—from head to toe."

Yes, please.

He straddled her, bracing his hands on the bed, he leaned down and captured her mouth. His tongue stroked hers, tangled and played, and took her deep. She moaned through the passionate kiss and wrapped her arms around his neck.

He broke the kiss and whispered against her lips, "Arch your back."

She lifted her back off the bed, allowing him to unclip her bra from beneath. Then he grabbed the lace creation and sent it flying. He didn't waste another moment before his mouth took in her spiked nipple.

"Ah," she cried out when he laved and sucked on her swollen breasts. She loved everything he did to her. God, it felt so good, she wanted to cry. Emotion overwhelmed her.

She laced her fingers through Mac's soft brown hair while his mouth journeyed down her torso. She found herself flexing her hips, straining to bring her sex closer to his kisses.

Hooking two fingers around the lace waistband of her panties, he slowly slid them down her legs and yanked them over her heels. His hands stroked her legs, and he resumed his kissing and licking. He let out a burst of warm breath over her sex, and she sighed. With the very tip of his tongue, he gently swiped over and around her clitoris. After too few passes, his lips moved to her inner thigh causing her to whimper.

She felt his smile against her skin. Bastard.

He teased, kissed, and licked her sensitive skin ignoring her drenched sex. Her only sign of hope came when he gripped her thighs and spread them apart, exposing her swollen, achy lips to his fingers.

He danced one finger over her sex, spreading her juices up and down. Then his tongue joined in, massaging her clit softly. Too softly. She needed more. Even as his finger pushed into her channel, she moaned, "Mac."

He added a fraction more pressure and another finger. The beginnings of a tremor shook her body. The slowly built orgasm coursed through her with spectacular heat. She cried out. Amazing. For a brief moment, she forgot where she was.

Mac retreated and hovered over her. In her semi-conscious state, she felt him raise her legs and align his cock at her entrance. "Beautiful," he breathed against her lips before claiming them. Deep, warm, hypnotic.

She cupped the back of his head, as he slowly, gently pushed his way into her core. She arched her back and whispered, "Mac."

His movements were deliciously arousing, pushing against her walls—she might come again.

"Wrap those sexy legs around me, Angelique. I'm going to take you harder."

Yes!

She linked her ankles, negotiating her heels behind Mac and felt his hands grasp her hands, holding them over her head.

"You are mine to command," he growled.

His pounding increased speed and the intensity grew. He continued for some time, beads of sweat forming on his forehead.

Suddenly, he pulled out.

What?! "What are you doing?"

"You're not coming," he said between breaths.

"I will."

The softening of his eyes told her he recalled their sexual encounter in their bedroom months ago. It was in this position that she'd confessed she couldn't come.

He leaned forward to place a kiss on her lips. His head hovered a few inches from hers.

"Give me your right hand." She moved both arms, to bring them by her sides.

"Uh-uh. Just the right. Keep this other hand overhead."

Another surge of heat shot through her at the thought of what he planned.

He laid her right hand on her thigh. "Show me what you like. Show me what gets you off."

Blood shot to her face. She'd never masturbated in front of Mac before.

"I, . . . I already came."

"You're stalling, my little minx. I want to see you pleasure yourself. I'm going to watch you make yourself come." And with that he pushed both her legs off him and apart, waiting on her. Heated eyes held her gaze, not backing down.

Oh, geez. She had to do this because Lord knew she needed release.

She slid her finger through her slit to gather some wetness, then slowly she circled her clit and sighed at the sensation. Her eyes fluttered closed as she allowed the sensations to grow. She felt Mac's hands stroke her thighs, and his sweet words enticed her.

In a short time, she broke through and her second orgasm gradually rose to the surface. She felt Mac hover over her and breathe against her neck, "Don't stop."

He kissed her neck and slowly slid into her. And to her surprise, the sensation only intensified her climax. She cried out as he pushed fully into her at the same time. Then after several pumps of his hips, Mac released with a grunt, muttering "Angelique" aloud.

He collapsed over her, holding most of his weight on his forearms.

God, that was so good.

After their breathing settled some, he pulled out, yanked off her heels, and rolled onto his back beside her. In the past, he might have fallen asleep or simply kissed her goodnight. Now, he held her hand and said in a low tone, "Beautiful."

She smiled to the ceiling then turned his way. "That

was amazing."

He gripped her hand, brought it to his mouth, and kissed the back. "It was."

They lay for several minutes, sated and content. At which point, Angie questioned herself, what now? They'd had sex, should she go? What were his expectations?

She'd packed a bag in case Mac wanted her to spend the night, and told the boys she would be home in the morning. She'd made it the clear that there were to be no friends over. No shenanigans.

Before she could think any more about it, Mac rose off the bed, shut off the light and returned, pulling the sheet and cover over her. Then, he slipped in and took a hold of her waist, turning her to spoon against his front.

Ah, there was her answer. He wanted her to stay.

"Sleep," he whispered in her ear.

And she was more than happy to spend the night with him. Words could not describe how amazing she felt—from the sex, to being in Mac's arms, to his sweet words, all of it. This side of Mac was impressive, surprising, and . . . she didn't know what. She couldn't find the words. It was like she was falling in love with him all over again.

CHAPTER TWENTY

After some of the most mind-blowing sex Mac and Angie had ever had, Mac couldn't sleep. He dozed for about an hour, but he wanted her again.

God, she was remarkable. He'd never seen her like this before. Of course, he'd never acted this way before either.

When he'd planned this night with Angie, the thoughts of their accidental sex episode in his office replayed in his mind. He was commanding and domineering over her. In an unexpected way, he liked it.

It was one thing to be authoritative at his job. It was to be expected. However, in the bedroom—in a relationship— it was another thing altogether. He and Angie were equals.

Well, he liked it and clearly so did she.

In an effort to create more hot sex, he'd decided he would command her tonight. And how well it had worked! Lying in the hotel bed in the dark, he began to get hard again.

Slowly, he slid his hand over Angie's hip. He heard a low moan pass her sleepy lips.

He didn't relent. He worked his hand up the side of her body and across the front of her torso to her belly and slowly to her breasts.

Her breathing increased tempo. She was awakening to his subtle actions.

As his hand caressed her breast, he kissed and nipped at her neck. His growing erection pushed against her ass, and feeling her small hip movements against him caused it to harden more.

"Mac," she breathed.

"Angelique, I want inside you so badly my cock aches. I need you good and wet before I slide in."

She groaned as he slid his hand down her front to her mons. Gently he slipped his finger over her clit and dipped between her folds. Her wetness had started to accumulate. She reached behind them and cupped his naked ass.

He bent his knee, sliding it between her legs to raise her top leg off the bed. "Keep this here, baby, so I can get to your delicious pussy."

Her breath hitched, but she didn't move a muscle. She allowed herself to be open to him and his desires. He slowly worked wide, long circles over her sex, all while kissing and licking her neck and shoulder. He shifted his body to allow his cock to align under her pussy. Working his hips back and forth, he gathered some of her wetness on his cock.

She sighed as he continued to stroke his cock and fondle her clit. She arched her back, and he knew shortly she would be ready for him. He wanted her more than ready. He wanted her panting with need. When he drove into her, she would be ready for an orgasm. *Aching* for him to give her an orgasm.

She warmed to his touch and her face showed a light sheen of perspiration. Soon.

"Mac," she said, her voice straining.

He positioned his body to align his cock at her entrance. "Hands on the headboard, Angelique."

She did as he told her and stretched her arms overhead to brace herself against the headboard. He gently separated her swollen, wet lips with his fingers and pushed himself into her wet channel. He groaned with her. She felt absolutely amazing.

Her inner muscles spasmed and he nearly came right then. Regaining control, he pistoned in and out in a timed manner—not too slow, not too fast. A glance at Angie's face, he could see her eyes were shut, her mouth was gapped, and her cheeks flushed. She looked positively beautiful.

He reached again to massage her clit, hoping all his efforts would bring her to orgasm. She deserved an orgasm. She deserved to orgasm every time.

Her panting became louder, as did his, and her clit swelled. He knew she was close.

"Oh," she whimpered.

He increased his pace fractionally, and commanded his body to wait for its release.

Then, he felt the tug of her vaginal muscles pull on his cock. The slow build of her orgasm.

"Yes, baby. You feel so good," he cajoled her.

"Ah," she cried out and threw her head back.

His thrusts increased, and although it became harder to focus, he kept circular movements over her clit.

She cried out again, and he didn't know if that meant her orgasm reached a climax or she had another one. All he knew was he couldn't hold on any longer. He released with a loud grunt and murmured at her back, "Angie."

Time passed as they regained their breaths, and gingerly Mac slipped out. He quickly grabbed a washcloth and wetted it with warm water.

He returned to a sated, naked, and sexy Angie, on her side, just as he'd left her.

"Let me wipe some of this," he said as she glanced over her shoulder.

She lifted her leg and let him wipe her skin.

"Mmm," was all he heard.

Then he heaved the washcloth back into the bathroom, watching it land on the tile floor. He yanked the sheet and cover back over them and spooned her from behind.

"Amazing," she breathed.

"You're amazing," he replied. "Sleep, baby."

He held her until her breathing deepened, and he knew she'd gone back to sleep.

Mac was a man on top of the world. He wouldn't count

his victory yet, but he knew after this night, he'd made strides to getting Angie back. Elation filled him to the core. The love of his life was coming back, and nothing else mattered.

Angie awoke decadently sore. She rolled onto her back and stretched. She felt tight and used and wonderful. Some of the best sex she'd ever had, was right there in that opulent hotel and that luxurious bed.

She tipped her head to Mac's side of the bed. Her heart plummeted. He was gone.

One glance at the bathroom, and the door was wide open with no lights on. Her sight moved to the chair. All his clothes were gone.

Why would he leave?

Tears pricked at the backs of her lids, until something caught her eye. She lifted her head and noticed a single red rose laying on Mac's side of the bed. She lifted it to smell. It was just like the dozen he had sent to her office days before.

A card also rested on the mattress. She moved the sheet and lifted the card.

> *I want to see you again.*
> *Mac*

And he'd written his cell number on the bottom of the card.

She snorted. Like she didn't know his number. He was keeping the game going, and she loved it.

She clutched the card to her chest and collapsed back down on the bed. A sigh slipped passed her lips.

Maybe they could save their marriage after all. The small smile that pulled at Angie's lips grew. *Maybe.*

She glanced at the clock.

Oh shit!

She flew out of bed, searching for her clothes. She never slept until nine o'clock unless she was sick. *Shit!*

Robbie had basketball practice. How was she going to make it in time?

Dress on, she smoothed her hair and pulled it back into a ponytail. She searched for a toothbrush in her bag as she shoved her panties inside. Then she reached for her phone on the desk and trekked to the bathroom. The screen illuminated.

What? She had a text from Robbie.

> *Dad is taking me to practice, then Stuart. He said he hoped you had a good night and to enjoy your breakfast.*

Angie grinned. Did she have a good night? The best. And Mac had everything under control. But, what did he mean about breakfast?

No sooner had the thought passed through her mind

when someone knocked on the door.

"Room service," the voice called out.

Angie looked through the peephole to see a young man dressed in black pants, vest, and a white shirt pushing a tray of covered dishes. She opened the door, and the man pushed the cart inside.

"Good morning, Mrs. MacKey. I'll set your breakfast over here, okay?"

She nodded and watched him set the dishes, the pot of coffee, and a rose in a vase on the table. She reached into her wallet for a tip, and the man left with a smile.

Angie lifted the lids. *Oh my.* The smell of the blueberry pancakes hit her in an instant. Another plate held a veggie omelet with hash browns. Her mouth watered. On a smaller plate sat bacon and sausage patties. So much food. Frankly, after last night, she thought she could make a reasonable dent in the fare. Mac had picked all her favorites.

First things first—coffee. After several flavorful sips, she set the cup down and stripped out of her dress and bra. She pulled on a hotel robe and cuddled up in a chair, staring at the feast.

Mac's gesture was so thoughtful. Really thoughtful. The whole previous night was so well planned and enchanting. She let out a sigh before taking another sip. She loved everything he'd done, including now. She basked in the glow of happiness.

The next step was hers. She didn't think she could plan

something so grandiose in a short time, but she knew one thing--in public relations, the gesture could be big or small, it didn't always matter, as long as it happened.

She lifted her phone and began to type.

I want to see you again too. Care to come over for dinner tonight, say 6:00?

She reached for the pitcher of syrup and covered her pancakes. She'd consumed three forkfuls when her phone chimed.

Good morning! Love to. 6:00 is perfect. What can I bring?

She thought.

Morning! Nothing. I'll have everything ready. And actually, we'd better make it 7, since I'm now lounging in the hotel room, sipping coffee, completely naked.

She grinned as she waited for his response while munching on some bacon.

Oh, Angelique. If I were there right now, coffee would be the last thing on your mind.

She laughed into her cup. She loved the banter. It had been years since they'd flirted with each other like this. Life seemed to be turning around. And just in the nick of time.

After the text he'd received from Angie, he had only one thing on his mind. Mac felt like a damn hormonal teenager thinking about her.

He'd taken a gamble last night. An insane gamble. Shit, he told—didn't ask—told her he was going to fuck her. He demanded she get down on her knees and suck him. He spread her legs and told her to masturbate for him. *What the hell!*

He wasn't so sure if the roles were reversed he would have responded so . . . kindly. He probably would have told himself to go fuck off. But not his girl. She'd loved it. And so had he.

His gamble had paid off.

He had himself an invitation to dinner. Perfect. He couldn't have asked for anything better. Correction, an invitation to spend the night would top it off. He would have an overnight bag in the car, just in case.

He glanced down at his wristwatch. Robbie's basketball practice went for another thirty minutes. Then they'd hustle to Stuart's football practice. So far, the school's basketball team looked good. They could work on tightening their passing, but the coach was solid, so he'd have them ready for next Saturday's game.

The football team rocked the season so far. With only one loss and one regular-season game left to play, they were on track for the playoffs. Stuart had excelled and would undoubtedly be first-string receiver next year.

Mac couldn't be more proud of his boys. The separation between him and Angie had created a few waves—mostly dips in the grades—but they'd refocused. There was a chance the boys were secretly happy their parents weren't fighting anymore. Regardless, Mac had assured them he was not giving up on his marriage. He didn't know if that was a good idea, maybe it gave them false hope, but it was the truth. And after last night, his prospects were looking up.

Glancing over at Stuart, he observed his son's thumbs flying over the smartphone and a smile widen on his face. Looked very much like a text to his new girlfriend. Noelle was her name. Sweet as a cup of hot chocolate. Mac didn't think their relationship had turned physical, but he had a gut feeling if they continued dating, it could.

Mac scratched his jawline. Perhaps he should have a friendly conversation with his eldest about women. He'd already covered the birds and the bees, just as the school had, years ago. No, what he wanted to discuss was different, something the school would never cover. Pleasure to a woman required care and attention. Men were like microwave ovens, but women were like crockpots. Slow to warm, but they could stay hot for a while.

Mac would make sure his sons knew the phrase *women first* didn't just mean the order to board a lifeboat or cross a threshold. They would have a conversation Mac was truly coming to understand. A conversation that could potentially avoid the situation Mac and Angie found themselves in.

He wouldn't dwell on that at this point. He was turning this ship around, and that was a good thing.

Angie leisurely showered at the hotel, dressed in fresh clothes, and headed to the store. She got the ingredients she needed for paella, and on a whim, she ran next door to the home store and bought a new set of satin bed linens. God, they were incredibly soft and smooth. This would be a nice unexpected touch.

She thankfully arrived home to an empty house, ready to get to work. First, she unpackaged the linens, washed them, and after a gentle dry, she ironed them and made the bed. It might be presumptuous that she and Mac would break in these sheets, but ultimately it was her choice. And if tonight was anything like the previous, . . . then Mac would definitely be staying.

After she ran the vacuum and picked up stray shoes and socks, she noticed a text from Stuart. It appeared Mac had taken them out to a late lunch and would be dropping them off shortly.

She started on dinner so it could be ready whenever

they wanted to eat. The boys walked in as she pulled plates and silverware out of the cabinets.

Her breath stalled, wondering why Mac wasn't with them. "Hey, kids. Where's your dad?"

"Hi, Mom. He said he wanted to get cleaned up. I guess he's coming over for dinner?" Robbie asked with a twinkle in his eye.

"That's right. Please take your stuff off the stairs."

"Okay, Mom," they said in unison.

With dinner basically done and the wine chilling, she made her way to the bedroom. She clipped her hair on top of her head and jumped into the shower. The sweet smell of her body wash would be great for an intimate evening. She rubbed a light lotion over her body in the same scent. Then, she fished out some sexy lingerie, a fine knit sweater, and her best jeans that hugged her ass perfectly. After freshening her makeup, she felt ready for her *date*.

She shook her head and smiled at the mirror. It had been *years* since she'd felt giddy over a date. Her heart beat just a little bit faster these past few hours. She peeked down at her watch to see she still had thirty minutes before Mac would arrive.

She strolled out of the bedroom into the great room and no sooner did she get some background music on when she heard the boys wrestling upstairs.

"Boys," she called. "Boys!"

She heard some more grunts. "Yeah?"

"Break it up and get ready for dinner."

Some more thuds and grunts, and someone muttered, "Wimp."

"Let's go," she called in the most authoritative voice she could muster.

"Okay." And after a few beats she heard water running.

She opened the wine, because Lord knew she needed something to do. Something to distract her from her nervousness. The doorbell rang, and her breath hitched.

He was five minutes early. She opened the door to a sexy, smiling Mac. Her heart sank. He'd dressed in a deep navy suit with a crisp white shirt and cranberry striped tie. A tie she'd hadn't seen before, for that matter.

She wore jeans.

"Hello," he greeted her with a sultry voice.

"I'm wearing jeans," she stated the obvious.

He wiggled his eyebrows. "I see that."

She giggled and stepped back to let him in. "You look very handsome. Please come in."

His hand on her waist, he leaned forward and kissed her cheek which sent a shiver up her spine. "These are for you," he whispered into her neck. He presented a bouquet of lovely red roses. She loved red roses. These weren't the grocery store kind. These came from a florist.

"Thank you. They're beautiful." The gesture touched her deep inside. When was the last time he'd brought her flowers? She bit back the tears and covered her emotion with an over-exuberant smile.

CHAPTER
TWENTY-ONE

Mac followed Angie into the kitchen, and he couldn't help notice how amazing her ass looked in those jeans. He wanted desperately to palm those gorgeous cheeks. Fuckable. That was the best way to describe how his wife looked to him right then. But that would have to wait.

She lay the roses on the counter and cut the tips before arranging them in a vase of water. "I opened the wine. Would you like a glass? We're having paella."

"Yes. I'll get it." He reached for a stemmed glass and poured the chardonnay. "Where are the boys?"

"Upstairs. They'll be down in a minute."

"Great." Without missing another beat, he did what he'd been wanting to do since her text that morning. He set down his wine, then cupped his hands around her jawline and neck, and leaned close, smoothing his lips over hers before diving in. She leaned into the kiss, and he dove deeper.

They kissed for several seconds before they heard footsteps on the stairs. He groaned and broke the kiss. A prelude. She grinned, but didn't say a word.

"Hi, Dad," Stuart said. "What's for dinner, Mom?"

"Paella. Would you please set the table?" She pointed to the stack of plates.

"Sure."

"What can I do?" he asked.

"Nothing. Make yourself comfortable. Perhaps you'd like to take off your jacket."

He lifted an eyebrow for only her to see and mouthed *that's all?* Angie's eyes twinkled and she bit down on her lip.

Stuart set the table while Angie covered the green beans to steam.

"Hi, Dad," Robbie said as he walked into the kitchen.

"Hey." Mac felt utterly comfortable. He wanted to make sure he wasn't too comfortable—to the point of being complacent. If he was going to do this, to recommit to his marriage, he was going to do it right. But he missed being at home, his home, with his family.

The boys took a seat and Mac placed the wine bottle on the table.

"How did your practices go today, boys?" she asked.

"Good," they said in stereo.

As the four of them ate, the boys talked about their sports and updated Angie on upcoming games. Stuart's phone chimed.

"Stuart," Mac said in a stern voice. "No electronics at the table."

"Sorry, Dad, but Matthew just got his license this week." He paused to read more. "He wants to know if I want to go to a movie tonight." Then he looked up eagerly. "Can I go?"

This could be a very good thing, Mac thought. He glanced at Angie, and she shrugged a shoulder of indifference. "Where are you going and what time would you be home?"

Stuart texted his friend, and Robbie asked, "Can I go with you?"

Stuart rolled his eyes at his brother, but he typed more, apparently asking anyway. "We're going to the Cineplex and should be home by midnight."

"What do you think?" Mac faced her.

She looked at the boys, and replied, "I suppose it's okay."

"Can I go?" Robbie asked again, bobbing her head.

"Yeah," Stuart mumbled.

On their good news, they each shoveled another forkful of food in their mouths. They finished in half the time, cleared their plates, and went to gather their shoes and jackets.

Mac and Angie ate at a more leisurely pace. Noticing her wineglass was empty, he refilled it.

"Thank you."

"So, how has work been going for you?"

"Good. The initial market test of the men's line went

very well. Jarmon is eager to roll it out corporate-wide next year."

"Yeah? That is good news," Mac said with a nod.

"It is. Plus, we've got some new designers we're working with, and that's adding to the excitement. Otherwise, nothing new going on. Just the usual."

Nothing was "usual" when it came to Angie and her job. He could recall a thousand stories of her quietly, confidently going about her duties, graciously accepting accolades, and all the while chalking it up to *I'm just doing my job*. If she didn't love her job so much, he'd want to hire her.

Stuart called from the foyer. "Matthew's here."

Mac stood. "Hold up." He met his boys before they bolted out the door. "No horse-play. Don't distract him. Just because you're not going very far doesn't mean there can't be an accident." He looked them directly in the eyes. "Come home right after the movie."

"Alright, Dad." They walked out, Mac waved to Matthew, and locked the front door.

Peace and quiet. All alone with Angie.

Mac sat back down, across from Angie, and refilled his glass. She asked about his work, and he updated her on the concern about Frisco's escalated manufacturing costs. He told her about the recycled water project and how the idea came to him. "Broccoli water."

Her face froze. "You're kidding."

"No," he said with a shake of his head and a grin on his face. "Just goes to show you, inspiration can come from anywhere."

She chuckled. "Well, I hope it works for you."

"At the very least, we should be doing this anyway," he said with conviction. "The amount of water Frisco uses is *insane*. I'm surprised we haven't implemented some sort of conservation method before now."

She leaned further back in her chair and crossed her legs.

They chatted like the old days and polished off the bottle of wine. He reminded himself how good it felt, and how he needed to hold on to this. He couldn't do things like he'd done them in the past. He couldn't take his marriage for granted.

Not to mention, he'd had a taste of the single life, and it sucked. Sure, he could make it into something audacious, but that really wasn't him.

Angie rose from her seat to clear the table. He got up too. "I'll help you."

She paused and met his gaze, perhaps wondering if he was serious. She didn't say a word. Just smiled and nodded.

He loosened his tie, left it on the chair, and stacked plates from the table.

Working side by side in their small kitchen, moving next to Angie and behind her, was energizing. Again, her ass in those jeans caught his eye. Distracting. His cock stirred at the random thoughts he had of Angie, bent over the counter.

Fuck! He needed to do something about his libido.

With everything cleaned and put away, Angie hung up the towel, and asked him, "Shall we go see what movies are on TV?"

He stepped closer and shook his head. Her eyes went wide, and she smoothed her lips together.

He cupped the side of her face in his hand. "I've been watching you move all night in this hot little outfit. Your ass in those tight jeans. All I can think about right now is peeling them off you and taking you in this kitchen." His eyes motioned to the island. "Right on this counter."

She gasped. "The neighbors will see."

He placed a hand firmly over her ass and gave a squeeze. "Fuck 'em." And he really felt that way, but in fairness to her, he reached behind and flipped the light switches for the kitchen and the table area. The kitchen went darker, leaving only a family room table lamp on.

"Better?" He didn't wait for an answer before he pulled her close for a tongue kiss. She tasted like rich wine and felt hot as summer. Her arms looped around his neck and her breasts pressed against his chest. God, she felt good.

He slid a hand down her body, over the side of her breast. His thumb roamed over her puckered nipple. She was getting turned on, and he had more to do.

He pulled back from the kiss and moved to her jaw and

neck. Her head tipped to the side, allowing his lips to roam where they wished. She smelled sweet. Delectable.

His hands pushed her sweater up, exposing her breasts covered in an ultra-sheer lacy number. The sight of her areolas caught him off guard.

"Damn! That's hot." He pressed her to the counter, arching her back, and bringing her luscious breasts closer to his mouth. He leaned forward, kissed the tops of her breasts, and sucked a nipple into his mouth right through her bra. She gasped.

She braced her hands on the counter as he took the other nipple and played his tongue over the distended peak. "Delicious," he said over her breast.

His tongue coated her bra, then glossed right in the middle of her cleavage. She moaned.

He continued his journey down her soft, smooth stomach and worked loose her jeans' button and zipper. His cock strained against his briefs. Did she know what she did to him? Before he pushed the pants down, he stood.

She met his eyes, and he grabbed her wrist. He pulled her hand and cupped it over his cock. "Do you feel what you do to me, Angelique?"

Her face was flushed, and her lips parted. "Yes," she choked out.

He pumped into her hand a few times. It would be so easy to get carried away, like he had, many times before with her. And it couldn't always be about him. No.

He pulled her hand away, bringing it to his mouth, and kissed her palm.

"Turn around, my sweet."

She did as he commanded. Sliding his hands over her ass, she radiated heat. He knew she would be wet and getting ready for him.

With his fingers hooked in her jeans, he slowly peeled them down over her hips, and held them for her to step out of.

His vision traveled to her matching lacy thong. "Your ass looks great in these."

She looked over her shoulder down at him. "You think so?"

He stroked his hands up and down her legs, and leaned in to plant a kiss on her ass.

He simply nodded. From his crouched position, he pushed against her lower back, positioning her torso across the granite countertop. She pulled down her sweater and rested her belly on the cool counter. He used a finger to trace over her lace thong, making his way to her warm, wet core.

Keeping his left hand on her lower back, he slowly eased a finger under the lace to her slick sex, and heard her moan at the contact.

He was fucking hard as a rock knowing how turned on she became. He wanted to impale her, bury himself deep inside her. On the flip side, he loved building the anticipation in her. Making her wetter by the minute.

He hooked two fingers under the thong at her hips, and pulled the fabric down her legs. She stepped out of her panties. He pushed her legs wider, and kissed and licked the backs of her thighs. He made his way closer to her glistening center. Her musky smell turned him on, and without thinking about it, he covered a soft section of skin at the base of her ass with his mouth. He licked briefly then sucked hard.

"Ah," she called out.

He held the position for several seconds, then licked over the tender spot. Before she could say a word about the mark he'd left, he moved his tongue to her exposed, waiting clit. He flicked it gently and moved his tongue through her core.

"Mac," she groaned.

He repeated the motion, each time taking longer, spending move time over her swollen little bud. He felt her push back against his face as her breath hastened.

He reached with his right hand to undo his belt and fly. He wanted to be ready when she was. Then he pushed one finger into her channel while working her with his tongue. When he pushed in another finger and twisted, he felt a tightening of her vaginal muscles. He increased the speed and felt her hips gyrate slightly against his face.

"Don't stop. Please don't stop," she said, her voice breathy.

Not until you are coming on my tongue.

Mere seconds afterward, she came. Loud and sweet. He loved hearing her climax.

Before she spiraled down, he stood and drove into her hot channel. Her muscles gripped him eagerly. She felt like heaven.

He leaned forward to nibble at her neck. "Your pussy feels . . . so damn good."

He couldn't hold out any longer. He shot his load deep inside her and gently bit the crux of her shoulder.

Collapsing over her, he breathed hard.

"Mmm," she breathed. "That was so good."

"Definitely. I feel like a freaking teenager."

She chuckled.

He kissed her neck and said, "Hold on." He reached for some paper napkins. He handed her one and kept one to wipe off his barely relaxing erection as he pulled out.

After she'd wiped herself, he took her napkin and tossed them. They redressed. He glanced in her direction in awe of her. The moment was freakin' perfect.

She made eye contact and a small smile graced her face. She studied him.

"What?" he asked.

She took in a breath and exhaled. "It's different."

She was right. It was different—the sex, the romance, the emotion. And that's what he'd been working toward.

He stepped closer, took a hold of the back of her neck, leaning down to kiss her gently. "You're right. And things are going to change around here, whenever you're ready to let me move back in."

The expression on her face remained neutral, but the sparkle in her eyes was undeniable. He would chip away at the barrier she'd built around herself. He'd prove to her he'd changed—he was wiser. Things *would* be different between them going forward.

"C'mon. Let's check out the movie listings." He tugged at her hand.

He grabbed the remote while she flipped on the front foyer light. Instead of sitting in his recliner, as he'd always done, he sat on the sofa next to her. Again, he felt her body tense briefly. He'd surprised her, and that fact alone made him grin inside.

He flipped through some channels, paused a few times, and finally they agreed on a comedy. He got comfortable, mirroring her actions; he propped his feet on the coffee table, and laid his arm across the back of the sofa at her shoulders.

Angie was still aglow from the amazing, spontaneous sex they'd had in the kitchen. Now she sat on the sofa with Mac next to her. She thought she'd better pinch herself. Everything was going so great . . . for a second consecutive night.

Her teeth dug into her lip. She didn't want to get too excited. Disappointment could be right around the corner if things reverted back to the way they'd been for the last few years.

But tonight had been different. Mac was attentive and in tune with her needs. Her desires. It was as if a switch had flipped. Something had happened with Mac, but she couldn't be sure. Maybe it was from when they'd unintentionally had sex in his office. God, she prayed this was real. That this was truly going to last.

She loved Mac, and being with him, in this way, made her feel . . . whole.

As they watched the movie, laughing and chatting sporadically, Mac leaned forward and grabbed a hold of her feet.

"Wha—"

Mac pulled her feet onto his lap, and with a knowing grin, he began to massage them. She shifted her body and reclined to get more comfortable. One at a time, he kneaded the heels, arches, and toes.

"Mmm," she breathed out. What a tremendous sensation. So relaxing.

Before she let her eyes close, she caught sight of his grin. "You like?"

"I do. You're being so good to me."

After a few more moments, she felt his warm breath tickle her cheek. "You deserve to feel good, Angie." She opened her eyes to see his face mere inches from hers. His penetrating gaze showed only sincerity. "I took us for granted. Being without you taught me that lesson. I missed you."

Moisture gathered in her eyes.

"We have so much to work on, but I don't want to throw in the towel. I want to try harder. Bringing home the bacon and the occasional trinket from someplace I've been wasn't enough." He stroked the side of her thigh, not intending to turn her on, but as a sign of affection.

"I need to try harder, too. I felt a distance with you, and instead of working to close the gap, I pushed you away. I walled myself in," she confessed.

He reached his thumb to smooth a runaway tear off her cheek. "I've never stopped loving you. Even when we were screaming at each other," he grimaced, "I never stopped."

"I never stopped either." She pressed her lips together and exhaled. "I'm scared."

"I know, baby. I am too. We have to recommit." He laced his fingers through hers. "We can't take each other for granted." She nodded her agreement. "I can't live without you again."

He slowly leaned forward and captured her mouth with his. With his hand on her thigh, he shifted her under him. Her hands caressed up his chest and laced behind his neck.

After several minutes of necking, Mac broke the kiss, shifted her on her side, and maneuvered himself to lying down behind her. He snaked an arm around her waist and pulled her close.

His semi-hard erection nudged her backside, but she decided not to mention it.

They watched the beginnings of another movie and Angie began to doze. The past few months had been an emotional upheaval. Her body relaxed in Mac's arms; she felt warm and safe.

After some time passed, Angie felt Mac shift off the sofa. He hooked an arm under her legs and another under her torso. Her eyes flew open.

"Easy, baby. I'm taking you to bed. You need to rest. The boys will be home any minute. I'll wait up."

He laid her on their king-sized bed, slipped off her jeans, and covered her as he placed a peck on her cheek. She easily dozed off in the comfort of her bed.

At some point during the night, Angie heard Mac talking with the boys. Knowing they were home safe and sound meant she could sleep.

She felt Mac slip back into bed behind her and pull her close. He dropped a warm kiss on her shoulder. She sighed. She may have been half asleep, but one thing remained true. He was trying. He had said he wanted to recommit, and not take her for granted. He was giving her what she needed.

She had to find a way to show him how much she appreciated all his efforts.

She smiled inside as she drifted off into sensual, passionate dreams.

CHAPTER TWENTY-TWO

As Mac dug through the fridge for breakfast foods, he noticed some things had changed. Turkey bacon had replaced their usual brand. The eggs were organic. More vegetables filled the crisper drawers. He knew their diet hadn't been bad before, but from the looks of it, Angie had decided it could be better. He smiled.

Mac prepared breakfast, the image of Angie in his arms, bathed in soft satin, replaying in his mind. Those sheets were a pleasant surprise. He loved that she'd thought of him and planned something special.

As soft as the sheets were, they couldn't hold a candle to Angie. Her skin felt supple and warm to his touch. He could steep in the feel, the touch, and the smell of her. Their weekend together was unparalleled. Her writhing beneath his tongue, whimpering when his fingers entered her, and moaning when he drove balls deep into her.

He was mad with wanting her. It had been years since he'd felt this fucking good.

She must have smelled the brewing coffee, because

after just a few minutes she appeared in the kitchen.

"Good morning," she greeted him.

He smiled. She wore a fluffy fleece robe he'd bought for her several Christmases ago. Her hair was slightly disarrayed, and her eyes sparkled. She looked good enough to carry back to bed for several hours of love making.

And if he didn't have so much work to do, that's where they'd be heading.

"Good morning." He leaned down to kiss her cheek. "Coffee's ready. How do you feel about an omelet for breakfast?"

Her lips curved in the sweetest little smile. He knew what she was thinking: *He rarely makes breakfast.* Well, things were about to change. Plain and simple.

"An omelet sounds good."

She retrieved a cup from the cabinet and filled it. Then she reached for his cup and topped it off.

"Thank you."

He savored this quiet time together. Soon enough the boys would be up and the spell would be broken.

Once he served the eggs and bacon, they sat and chatted about nothing much over breakfast. He shared that he needed to head to the office for a few hours to knock some things off his list. He could sense something was on her mind. *Is she mad because I have to work on a Sunday?*

Finally, she spoke. "Mac, I've been giving it some thought." She brought her head up to meet his eyes. "Maybe you should think about moving back into the house."

The words were music to his ears. An answered prayer. He sat in silence for a while and then let his lips curve upward. "I'm making you an omelet again tomorrow, unless you'd prefer pancakes, or French toast, or scrambled eggs."

She grinned. "I'll take that as a yes. And you don't have to make me breakfast, but," she swiped her bottom lip, "I can see you're trying. I'll try harder, too, Mac. I want us to work on this marriage and the only way is together. I may be jumping the gun, but that's what my gut tells me."

He reached over, took her hand, and kissed the back gently. "I would love to move back in. I realized I'd stopped trying, and that's not happening again." He meant the words, and he hoped she believed him. "You cooked, cleaned, did most of the boys' school things, helped more with their homework, did the grocery shopping, and ran the errands. I promise to start sharing some of that load."

Tears welled in her eyes, and he wasn't sure if that was a good thing or not. Had he said too much?

He gets it. She wanted to cry for years of not being understood, of not having him hear her, and now his words were like a soothing balm on her heart. The tears gathered, unshed, until that last promise to share the load. She blinked and they streamed down her cheeks.

He swiftly wiped her cheeks with his thumbs and shifted closer. "Angie, don't cry."

A sob escaped.

"God, Angie. Tell me you're okay." He scooped her onto his lap, and wrapped his arms around her.

"I've waited to hear those words. Waited to feel this good. I want us to work. More than I ever realized." She sniffled.

"I'm sorry. I took you for granted. You'll never wonder again how much I love you." He placed his lips over hers and kissed her gently.

She cupped her hands to his face, kissing him back. He felt so good, and her body responded to him, to his kiss.

His tongue connected with hers and reignited the fire from last night. She felt his subtle bulge at her hip.

The kiss heated, and grew deeper. The low groan traveled from his throat to her belly, spreading a warmth to her limbs. A thrill raced through her knowing he was turned on because of her.

She shifted and felt his cock pressing into her side.

"Ang," he breathed into her neck.

"Mmm."

"Come with me. Shower." He pulled the sash of her robe loose.

She backed away, adding distance, and meeting his eyes. "Mac, you're crazy. There's no room for both of us."

His hand slipped under the fabric to find her completely naked. "Look. You're already ready." He grinned.

She grabbed his wrists and stood, scooting her bottom off his lap. As enticing as the idea of getting naked and wet with him was, it was *very* unrealistic. The boys were asleep upstairs.

He playfully narrowed his eyes. "Are you denying me?"

She bit on her lip. "Mac, maybe we—"

He didn't allow her to finish her thought. In a swift move, his hands cupped her face and his mouth over hers.

He claimed her, dominated her. His muscular body, the soft cotton of his T-shirt, brushed her sensitive, excited nipples.

"Arms around my neck, and legs around my waist, Angie," he commanded her without breaking their precious contact.

Oh hell. She swung her arms over his shoulders, holding on, while she lifted one leg. His arms slipped under her robe, clutched her ass cheeks, and hauled her up into his hold. She crossed her ankles behind him.

As he walked, he breathed into her neck, "You feel good against me, in my hands."

She smiled. "I still think you're crazy."

"Crazy for you." He set her down on the tile floor of their bathroom and turned the shower on full blast. He shed his clothes, and quickly yanked the robe from her body.

He was magnificently hard for her—muscles taut over his abdomen. His chest showed off the sculpted definition he worked at. Moisture collected at her sex, and the dull ache became distinctive.

With little hesitation, he opened the glass door, stepped back into the shower, and holding her hand, guided her under the hot spray. The confines of the space brought them close. Mac's hands roamed her wet body. He groaned.

She blinked the water out of her eyes, barely able to see Mac's lips close over hers. She closed her eyes fully and savored his tongue stroking hers.

His erection pressed against her low-stomach. She reached her hands between them caressed his swollen member. He moaned into her mouth.

His hands slid up her torso to fondle her heavy breasts. He whispered over her mouth, "Do you know how fuckable you are right now?"

She gasped at his words, feeling a new rush of liquid heat.

He grabbed her wrists and pulled them off him. "Turn and place your hands on the wall."

There was that commanding voice again. She hesitated the briefest of moments before she faced the wall, giving him her back. She didn't know what he had planned exactly, but she didn't care. She trusted Mac to make her feel good, and she couldn't wait another minute.

She heard him pop the top on her body wash as the water cascaded down her back. Then, she felt the warm wet washcloth glide down her back while his other hand held tightly to her hip. He stroked her slowly up and down, over her back, shoulders, hips.

"Spread your legs," he said, breaking her trance.

She gained stability in her stance as Mac squatted down to clean one leg at a time. It was only when she felt his left hand slide to her low belly that she knew what he wanted. He pushed against her, pushing her ass closer to his face.

She arched her back, giving him access.

"This ass is marvelous." She strained to hear him, his breath hot against her ass cheek.

He rained kisses over her cheeks, licking and nipping as his hands massaged the backs of her thighs. The ache built inside her, making her needy.

Touch me.

The washcloth ascended her right leg—calf, thigh, and stopping at the crack in her ass. With two hands, he pulled the edge of the washcloth taut and made his way to center. Leisurely, the cloth stroked her sensitive rear.

"Oh, God," she breathed. Her head fell forward. Mac stood and slowly, gingerly caressed her tight hole with the tingling washcloth.

"Arch more, Angie," she heard him at her ear.

She felt like—what?—a stripper, trying to put on a show for the audience. Mac didn't stop, and she was desperate to grab something, like the tile could serve as a sheet or blanket to bunch in her hands.

The warm, plush cotton brought her nerves alive in a

way she never thought possible. Sensations flooded her body, causing her legs to tremble.

"Turn around," he said as he removed the washcloth.

She wanted to moan in frustration.

While he loaded more body wash on the cloth, she glanced at his cock, standing at attention, looking delectable. She reached for him with her hand, and he moved back.

"Uh-uh. Hands on the wall."

"Mac, I want to touch you."

He stopped midway up the side of her torso. "I know, and you will. Right now, if you touch me, this will be over far too quickly." He leaned forward, placing a quick peck on her lips.

Her hands flattened against the tile. Mac caressed her torso and cupped her breasts with the washcloth. She moaned and arched into his touch, reveling in the feel, her eyelids fluttered closed.

"Mac."

His lips landed on her neck, kissing and licking in just that perfect way. His erratic breathing betrayed the calm in his movements.

She heard the washcloth drop to the floor, and she opened her eyes. His knee moved between her legs, nudging them open. At the same time, he grabbed her hands, stretching them over her head, pinning them to the wall.

"By now, I suspect you're dying for an orgasm. Is that

right, Angelique?" he asked in the same tone he'd used at the hotel.

His gaze locked onto hers, only his hands moved. Her wrists were transferred to one large hand while his free hand traveled down her torso to the tip of her breast.

"Yes," she breathed. "Please."

He tweaked her nipple, hard. When she cried out, he caught her gasp in his mouth, claiming her. God, his mouth, his tongue, felt like heaven.

He devoured her mouth as his fingers trailed down her belly to her mons.

He pulled back only long enough to say, "The next time I bring you in here, Angelique, I'm shaving every last hair from your luscious pussy."

His mouth swallowed her whimper. She would grant him anything right then. Anything.

The tip of his finger slid slowly down her sex and glossed between her lips.

"You are so fucking wet."

She whimpered again. The anticipation was more than she could bear.

He dipped slightly and gathered her juices spreading some over her engorged clit. *Finally!*

He played in small, gentle circles, occasionally dipping his finger inside her. She couldn't think. She couldn't breathe. She broke the kiss and gasped for air, water spilling over her face. Her hips bucked against his fingers.

He increased the speed and pressure over her clit. She bucked again, and Mac's hands gripped her wrists tighter.

"Wider, Angelique."

She spread her legs as wide as the space allowed, and he drove two fingers deep inside her.

"You feel incredible." His fingers moved with singular focus.

She panted. "I'm close, Mac." *So close.*

Then she felt three fingers dive into her channel as his thumb worked her clit.

"Unh." She closed her eyes, her climax rising to the surface to surge through her.

She cried out. Mac maintained his rhythm for several moments before he released her hands and lifted her thigh to his hip. Bending at the knees, he aligned his cock at her entrance and drove in, lifting her off the floor.

"Fuck."

She quickly wrapped her arms around his shoulders and held on. His pounding rocked her against the cold tile. She dropped her lips to his neck, sucking and kissing his delicious, masculine skin.

As he started to climax, she gently bit at the crux of his neck. He growled and pulled her hair, bringing her lips to connect with his.

His pumping slowed until he pulled out. She felt relaxed and energized at the same time—so alive.

"Damn, woman. That was hot," he breathed into her

wet hair, holding her close. His heart pounded against her chest.

"Absolutely."

He kissed her one last time before releasing her thigh and straightening his spine.

She exhaled a quivering breath. "Let's wash and get out of here before the kids come down." She couldn't help wanting to keep some decorum, at least where her boys were concerned.

"Okay."

She washed and rinsed her hair, and slipped out to give Mac more room.

Hot. That was the only word she could use to describe the sex she was now having with Mac. What an amazing weekend. The last time they'd had sex like this they'd been in their twenties.

Everything felt new. She'd fallen in love all over again. With her husband. They were committed to making their marriage work. *But how do we do that?*

A small pit formed in her stomach. Truly, beyond sex, what had improved? What had they done differently? And if it was that easy to *fix* wouldn't it be that easy to fall right back into bad habits?

Mac stepped next to her, wrapped a towel around his waist, and pulled a comb out of his bag. He caught her eyes in the reflection of mirror.

"What are you thinking about?" he asked.

She must have looked worried. She nibbled the inside of her cheek. Truth. He deserved only the truth from her.

She turned to face him directly. "I was thinking how amazing this weekend has been. I love the way you touch me. The way you make me feel." His eyes softened hearing her words. "I'm nervous it won't last."

Angie's confession hit him blindside. Mac appreciated her honesty, and that same thought had crossed his mind once or twice. He hadn't anticipated talking about it.

Mac took in a breath, set his comb on the vanity, and held her hands. "We work on it every day. We don't take each other for granted. We may not have sex like this every weekend—I sorta think we are making up for lost time." A smile tugged from her lips. "But if we both agree to try, to commit, it will be good for us. We won't repeat the last several years. We can be better. We are smarter for what we went through."

"We work on it every day," she repeated his words.

"But Ang, you have to talk to me." Her eyes went wide. He stepped closer, snaking his arms around her waist. "You have to tell me what you like. What you don't. I won't know otherwise. Can you do that?" He raised an eyebrow.

She nodded as if shy. "I can do that. I haven't done a very good job of that in the past. Although I think you know quite a lot about what I like." All her white teeth showed in her beautiful smile.

"I'm learning." He leaned to kiss her swollen red lips, more gently than before. "I'll get dressed and see if the boys are up. Take your time."

He threw on some jeans and a comfortable knit shirt. It didn't matter too much what he wore when he went to the office during the weekend.

He strolled into the quiet kitchen and poured another cup of coffee. Looked like the boys were still asleep. Teenagers seemed to sleep a lot. He smirked.

Angie was right on many levels. It was good now. So fucking good. And they'd have to work to keep it that way. He didn't have all the answers, or know what they should do every step of the way. But he knew one thing for sure. He wouldn't repeat what he'd been doing all these years. As Ryan had pointed out, what he'd been doing wasn't working.

He loved his wife. Working to save their marriage—make her happy, make her feel good—didn't seem like work at all. A picture of her in the throes of an orgasm flashed in his mind. *Especially* making her feel good.

After about twenty minutes, Angie emerged from the bedroom. Shortly thereafter, the boys came down. They didn't seem surprised to see him, but they certainly seemed happy.

Over their breakfast, he asked about their plans for the day, and they both replied, "Homework."

Angie said she had some cleaning and grocery

shopping to do. "What would you like for dinner?"

That question was damn-near music to his ears. She'd included him in their activities, their day. Months of separation made every moment with his family feel like progress.

"I don't think I have a preference. Surprise me," he said with a grin on his face. "I'll run to the office for a few hours, then to the apartment to grab some things."

Both boys jerked their heads his way.

"Are you moving back in, Dad?" Robbie asked.

He glanced at Angie, leaning against the kitchen counter, and her eyes sparkled. "Yes, your mom and I decided to give it a try. Are you alright with that?"

"Yeah." Robbie, first for any new adventure, nodded as his too-long hair flopped in his face.

"Of course," Stuart agreed. Always the more responsible one.

"Good. Well, let's have a productive day." He rose from the kitchen table and strolled toward his glowing wife. "I'll be back around four, and I can help you with dinner."

He reached up with one hand and cupped the back of her neck, angling her head toward his. Then he sealed his lips over hers with a kiss to carry her through her day. Their tongues danced, and she leaned into him. Her body flush to his felt amazing. He could take her again—easily—but then he'd never get out of there.

Nearly breathless, he brought his lips to her forehead.

"See you soon, sweetheart."

She smiled up at him. "Okay."

"Get your homework done, guys. San Fran plays Saint Louis tonight. It should be a good game."

"Okay, Dad." Robbie gave him a thumbs up.

"See you later."

"Bye," his family called after him.

Mac couldn't seem to wipe the grin from his face. Not that he wanted to. His weekend with Angie had gone better than he'd planned or expected. They were on the right track. No doubt about it.

Using his keycard, he entered the office building and took the elevator to the twenty-sixth floor. He unlocked his office door. As much as he hated coming in on the weekends, he also loved it. The whole floor was quiet. He could think and work more efficiently without interruptions. Getting ahead of the curve would be good since end-of-year was rapidly approaching.

No sooner had his computer come alive when Camille appeared at his doorway.

"Hi, Mac. I didn't know you would be in."

"Hi. Yeah, trying to get some work knocked out before year-end."

"Yes, of course. I was heading to get myself some coffee. Can I get you a cup?"

"Thanks. I'll take—"

"I know," she cut him off, "French roast or Sumatra,

black."

He smiled to hide his surprise. "That's right." How the hell did she know that? Well, obviously, through their years of working together, she was observant.

He dug into his reports when several minutes later Camille appeared, holding two cups of coffee.

"Thanks." Camille took a seat across from his desk. He stopped typing, not sure why she was staying.

"You're welcome. So, how's it going?" The scent of her rich perfume filled the space.

She leaned back in the chair and crossed her denim-clad legs. He couldn't imagine how comfortable that position was considering the tightness of her jeans. He also noticed her snug, deep V-neck sweater showing off an abundance of cleavage. He wouldn't fault her; it was the weekend. Perhaps she had a date later.

"Good." He really didn't want to engage her in conversation. Hadn't he just thought how productive working in silence was?

"You seem to be doing well. You look good." Her smile glimmered.

What? "Thanks."

"How much work do you have?"

"A few hours."

"Me too." Then she leaned forward as if to rise, but she didn't. Instead she gave him a decent view of her voluptuous breasts and a hint of black lace beneath. She toyed with a gold chain at her neck. "So, how about after we're done here we go grab a drink? Or something?"

And there it was, as clear as Ketel One vodka. His heart thudded in his chest, and not in a good way. Camille was a woman with goal—and that goal was him. Mac had been there before. *Dammit!* Best thing he could do was squash it before it got out of hand. He *would not* go down that road again, for the love of God.

"Camille, I cannot go for a drink with you. I will be going home afterward, to my wife."

"Oh, I wasn't trying to imply—"

"You weren't?" He cut her off with a raised brow.

Silence. "I had heard you had moved out."

What the fuck?! "Well, that's ancient history." He embellished. "My wife and I have reconciled, and I couldn't be happier." No embellishment there. He held her gaze making sure his words sunk in clearly and succinctly.

Camille straightened in her chair, and after just a beat, she rose. "My apologies. I didn't mean to cross any lines between us. I certainly hope this doesn't affect our working relationship."

"Not in the least." He hoped. Furthermore, he hoped she wouldn't turn into a kind of woman scorned. "Have a good day. See you later."

She took the hint and left his office.

What the fuck? He should have seen it coming. Camille hadn't been acting like herself lately. The big question, was this conversation enough to squelch any further advances? Did Camille understand they had zero chance of a relationship?

He rubbed his fingers on the side of his forehead. He needed to move beyond this, to focus. Reports and spreadsheets awaited him. And the sooner he got it knocked out, the sooner he could go home.

CHAPTER
TWENTY-THREE

H er heart raced with the adrenaline coursing through her veins. The idea came to her that Tuesday morning after the kids went off to school—the perfect idea on how to repay Mac for their wonderful weekend. For never giving up on them.

It had been two days since Mac had moved back in. He'd hustled out of the house that morning telling her he had an early meeting, and he would see her for dinner. He'd kissed her soundly, awakening the butterflies in her stomach. The sexy, sultry smile on his lips would stay in her mind all morning, in the shower, over breakfast.

She dressed for work— *and* her plan. And boy, would it be good.

Angie strolled past Nicci's cube. "Good morning."

"Good morning to you. Wait. What are you wearing?" Nicci stood, her eyebrows raised.

Angie glanced down at her black pencil skirt. The sleek garment had been stashed in the back of her closet, patiently waiting for her to fit into it again. When she'd slipped it on that morning, she'd felt so pretty that she'd smiled at her reflection—on top of the world.

"Oh, this? It's not new. I bought this years ago." She grinned at Nicci.

"You look hot. The whole ensemble looks great on you."

"Thank you."

Nicci hitched a hip on the side of Angie's desk as Angie booted up her computer. "So things are still good on the home front?" Nicci dropped her voice a fraction, prying for details.

Angie leaned in. "Is it possible to have too many orgasms?"

Nicci's chuckle filled the space and her eyes glowed. "Nope. Not at all. In fact, studies have shown it adds years to your life."

"Well, in that case I'm living to *two* hundred."

They laughed together. "Good for you. You deserve it." Nicci rose, straightening her pant leg. "Now, we have thirty minutes before the monthly staff meeting. They've brought us boxes to pack up so they can move us the day after tomorrow." She pointed at the tower of boxes across the hall. "Do you want me to grab you a cup of coffee?"

"No, thanks. I'm good." *I'm high on life right now.*

The staff meeting dragged. She glanced at her watch—

eleven thirty. She'd wanted to be on the road by now. It would take her twenty-five minutes to get downtown to Mac's office, with no delays, and then find parking.

Finally, Jarmon adjourned the meeting. She leaned over to whisper in Nicci's ear, "I've got something I need to take care of during lunch. I might run over an hour."

Nicci tucked away her papers and took off her reading glasses. "Yeah, no problem. I got ya covered."

"Thanks." Angie grasped her binder and headed to her desk. She slung her purse over her shoulder and prayed Mac hadn't left for lunch yet.

Mimi popped her head into Mac's office. "Mac, I'm heading out for lunch. Okay?"

"Sure." He'd be a few steps behind her, assuming his conference call went well.

Mac had planned a call with his managing directors to touch base on year-end numbers. It would be eight o'clock in Hawaii, and Mac knew that was as early as he could comfortably get away with.

Later that afternoon, he would conference with Australia and New Zealand. The following day, he would connect with his European counterparts, then Asia-Pacific shortly thereafter.

Jarring him from his thoughts, Angie stood at his door wearing a pale pink silk button-down blouse, hip-hugging straight skirt and fuck-me high heels. From head to toe, every inch of her looked perfect. Mac suddenly could think of nothing but rolling around naked with her for the rest of the day.

Mac circled his desk and greeted her with a quick kiss on the lips and flashed her a sexy smile. "This is a pleasant surprise. To what do I owe the pleasure?"

"Hi, Mac. I'm glad I caught you before you went to lunch."

He stepped back and motioned to an extra chair. "Have a seat."

She pushed the door closed. "I hope I'm not disturbing you. Do you have lunch plans? I thought we could have lunch together." *Eventually.*

She willed her racing heart to calm. Why was she so nervous? This was Mac, for goodness sake.

"Sure. I have a conference call, but it shouldn't take long. Then we can grab lunch," he nodded.

Oh, crap. He had a conference call. She should call it off and settle for lunch only.

Don't chicken out now, she scolded herself.

She smoothed her lips together and turned to lock the door. "Terrific. In the meantime, I think I left something here."

His eyebrow rose and he scanned the room. "Oh?"

She tipped forward, grabbed the hem of her skirt, and shimmied it up over her hips.

"Oh, fuck."

She flashed him. Standing in the middle of his office, sans panties and completely denuded, she flashed her husband. A quick glance down the front of his trousers told her he approved.

She'd shaved herself completely bare that morning, knowing he'd appreciate that. Then before leaving her car to come inside, she'd slipped her panties off. Her cheeks warmed at her brazen moves.

"You look fucking amazing," he said in a deep voice, glancing down again.

"You like it?"

"I love it," he said as he closed the distance and pulled her flush into his rock hard body, her sex brushing against his wool trousers. His large warm hand cupped her ass cheek. "I have to admit, I'm not sorry you lost your panties. You should definitely look around—" The phone ringing cut him off. "Shit. I have to take this."

"So take it," she smiled like a Cheshire cat. "I'll start on the floor and work my way up."

His eyes narrowed as his head tipped back. "Be good," he warned. There was no stopping now.

He strode back to his chair and brought the phone to his ear. "MacKey," he answered. "Is everyone on?"

His tone may have shown focus on the phone, but his eyes tracked her movements. She set her purse on the chair opposite his desk and lowered herself to the floor. On all fours, she crawled slowly, pretending to search for misplaced panties. She didn't bother to lower her skirt. She *was* brazen.

She could feel his eyes on her, on her bare ass sashaying across his office floor.

He cleared his throat. "Excellent. Ben, let's start with you. Do you think Cal-Mark will take advantage of the end-of-year volume pricing we offered them?"

Angie vaguely heard murmured conversation from the other end of the line as Ben responded. She crept closer to Mac's side of the desk, stopping at his feet. He pushed back, wearing a grin, and she peered under his desk for her "missing panties."

She looked up at him, giving the best befuddled face she could, and shrugged a shoulder.

The twinkle in his eyes told her he was completely amused. Time to pull out the big guns.

She glanced down at his bulging crotch and made a show of licking her lips.

His eyes widened. He spoke into the phone, "I see. Well, keep me posted. That sale would be a great win. Especially now. Carl, would you update us on your region? How is everyone faring the snowstorm?"

Silence. Phone still to his ear, and his eyes never leaving hers—caution in his intense stare. Shifting her weight and adjusting her skirt, she slowly lifted her hands, one to each of Mac's legs, and stroked his calves. All while watching him watch her.

"Excellent. Circle back around with Logistics. Let's make sure we fill those shelves as soon as trucks can get back in there." His voice had a raspy edge now.

Her hands moved outside his pants and slid over his knees up his thighs. His muscles flexed under her palms. She gently pushed his strong thighs and scooted closer in between them.

"Uh . . . Allie, how is the rollout in Freshie's southeastern region?"

Mac shifted in his plush chair. Clearly, things were getting tense below the waist.

Sliding her hands over his swollen cock, she stroked him several times before carefully removing the leather belt from its buckle. She watched a tight shake of his head, but he didn't stop her. She eased open his fly and pulled down his briefs enough to let the head of his cock free. The sight was mouthwatering. He wanted her as much as she wanted him.

She wasted no time circling the exposed head with her eager tongue.

"Mm-hm," he blurted out as his breath caught. "I agree, and they love being first to market. Okay, Allie, send over the details as soon as you get them from the team. Good job."

Angie tugged against his briefs to expose more delicious cock. She needed more. He stirred, allowing her to pull his clothing where she wanted it.

"Lastly, Joshua. Whaddya got?" His breath sounded rapid.

Her mouth wholly closed over him and slid down. He gripped the back of her head. If he thought for one moment he could stop her, he was sorely mistaken. She smiled to herself and worked his cock like it was their last day on earth. She licked, stroked, and sucked him. She fisted him in concert with her stretched lips pleasuring him.

He clutched her hair and neck harder. The pain raced through her scalp, but it wasn't enough to stop her. She loved making him feel good. Perhaps she'd never realized that fact until now. Or maybe she simply forgot how good it felt to give him pleasure.

At the same time, her sex wept with need. Her thighs gripped closed. She clasped her hands at his hips to keep him in place.

"Uh-huh," he managed to get out. He lifted the receiver away from his mouth, his breathing ragged.

She continued her assault. Finally, he dropped his head back, pulsed his hips upward and exploded into her mouth. She drank him in. A small groan escaped and Mac quickly turned it into a cough for the listeners' sake. A glance up at her husband's handsome face showed him in absolute nirvana.

He took in a breath. "Yes, that'll work, Joshua. Good job." He met her square in the eyes. The heated look told her she was in some kind of trouble. Oh yeah.

"Well, folks, I think we are on track. Keep up the good work and we can close out the year up."

Several short moments passed and Mac hung up the phone. He stared down at her with an incredible fire.

"Get up. Lift that skirt again and sit your ass on my desk." He pointed firmly. "We will eat lunch after I eat you, Angelique."

Her insides clenched and her stomach flipped. She stood and he rose too, pulling her close to cover her mouth with his. He ravished her in a passionate kiss. After a few beats, he released her. "I can taste myself on you. Now sit."

She smiled at his declaration. Warmth spread throughout her body.

Angie hiked up her skirt and sat in the center of his desk before him. He situated his pants and reattached his belt. He sunk back in his chair, pointed to the chair arms, and commanded, "Feet up."

She placed a foot on each armrest of his leather chair— spread out for him. He looked at her like he wanted to devour her. He pushed her legs farther apart and said, "I can see how wet you are."

He dragged a finger through her core, and she bowed at the sensation. "You've been a bad girl, coming in here, blowing me while I'm trying to work." His voice was deep and thick.

He twirled a digit a tiny inch in her channel, teasing.

He leaned forward and blew a gust of breath over her sex, causing her to shudder. "I should leave you here and tease you for an hour without an orgasm."

His tongue made a pass up her core to the hard nub. She flexed.

"Ah."

"But you have also made me very happy, parading this sexy pussy for me." Another lick.

She leaned back and braced her hands on the desk with a whimper.

"Did you shave your wet pussy for me, Angelique?" He pushed his finger completely inside her.

"Yes," she said on an exhale.

"And you decided to come down here and show me." Two more licks.

"Yes." Her breathing came in pants.

"Well, this beautiful sight makes me hard." Three more licks and a swirl with his tongue.

Oh, God.

"I'm going to make you come right here, baby. Then tonight I'm going to fuck you with all the lights on so I can get my fill of your gorgeous naked body. Do you understand?" Another finger pushed into her.

"Ah. Yes, Mac. Yes. Please." She spread her legs as far as they could go. She needed release so badly. She'd agree to anything.

He gave her what she wanted. His warm, wet tongue

worked her clitoris while his talented fingers pulsed rhythmically in and out of her dripping channel. When he curved his fingers to caress her g-spot, she came hard—half in reality, half out. She felt a liquid release and restrained an outcry because she was in his office, but God, did that feel good.

She panted and let her head fall back. He pulled his fingers out and wiped her with his handkerchief. After he finished, she rose upright and removed her feet from his chair. He stood, and cradling her face, he took her mouth with his. She held onto his shoulders and pressed her body against his. He kissed her long and hard, and their flavors commingled.

He pulled back an inch. "How do you feel?"

She smiled, her head still foggy. "Good. Really good. How do you feel?"

"Best fucking blow job ever."

She released a chuckle. "I'm glad you liked it."

He held her close for several more moments, then said, "Let me shut this down, and we can go grab some lunch."

She hopped off the desk while he fussed with his computer. She fixed her attire the best she could. The wrinkles in her skirt were just going to have to stay there. Not much could be done at this point. She hunted down her compact mirror and fixed her hair and makeup. The flush on her face made her look young and . . . happy. She'd fallen in love all over again. Plain and simple. Of course, there was no denying the post-sex euphoria.

"Ready?" His voice grabbed her attention as he held open the door for her.

He took her hand and led her to the elevator.

As the elevator doors were about to close, a tall, blonde woman and a shorter man with glasses dodged between the doors before they closed completely. The woman was insanely gorgeous—tall, shapely, and a smile to envy. Her clothes were designer and her makeup was perfect. The man sounded out of breath.

"Hi, Mac."

"Camille. Reynold. This is my wife, Angie," Mac announced, then turned and smiled at his blushing bride. "Angie, this is Camille, our VP of Finance, and Reynold, our comptroller."

Angie smiled and nodded. "Nice to meet you both."

"You work at l'Amour Lux, right?" Camille asked.

Angie's lips curved. "Yes, that's right."

The elevator stopped on eleven and two people got on.

"I love that store." Her hand bent at the wrist, her polished fingertips tapping her chest. "So many great styles. Unique but still mainstream. Very appealing."

"I'm so glad you like it. Thanks for being a customer."

Mac leaned down, close to Angie's ear, but not to whisper. "Sweetie, don't we need to run by your car before heading out to lunch?"

She jerked her head in his direction, eyes rounded. Her rosy cheeks flushed to a deeper shade. Mac had a hard time scolding himself when she looked so damn beautiful.

"Uh, yes. That would be great. Thank you."

They all exited the elevator. Mac's hand clung to Angie's, directing her to the parking garage.

"Why did you say that in front of everyone?" she hissed as she yanked his arm.

"What?" He glanced her way.

"You know what. You practically announced I wasn't wearing panties."

He stopped and pulled her close. His strong arm rounded her waist. He couldn't say exactly why he'd mentioned that in the elevator. Perhaps it had to do with Camille being an audience. Or because Angie looked so gorgeous after coming so hard in his office, he wanted to show the world she was his and always would be.

"Four people isn't exactly *everyone*. But your point is taken. I am so fucking happy, I want the world to know. I will refrain from embarrassing you in front of others from now on. I apologize."

Her mouth gaped.

He did a secret victory dance at leaving her speechless.

"Thank you. I . . . um, appreciate it."

He kissed her briefly. "Let's go."

CHAPTER
TWENTY- FOUR

After Angie discreetly slipped her thong back on, Mac held her hand while they walked to a little Italian bistro three blocks from his office. It had been years since they'd had lunch together during the week. And he fucking loved it.

She looked happier than he'd remembered seeing in a long time.

As they munched on bread dipped in olive oil, Angie opened a new topic. "Mac, I want to talk about the house."

"Okay, what would you like to talk about?" He'd suspected it would only be a matter of time before Angie wanted to talk about the house they'd probably outgrown years ago. He didn't mean to be stubborn about the issue, but considering he'd been traveling the majority of the time, what need was there for a bigger house? With his recent promotion, that excuse was now out the window.

She blotted the corner of her mouth with the napkin. "It really is too small for the four of us. When the boys were babies or toddlers, it was fine. But now personal space, storage—it all feels too crowded. I want to look into either selling it and moving into a larger house or remodeling and expanding what we've got."

He nodded. As much as he hated the idea of packing and moving, he could see the benefit of getting something larger all around. A place where every room was more spacious. The flip side was, their lot could hold a larger home. Without moving, they could bump out a wall and expand the living space, and possibly upstairs too. He knew, easier said than done, but the increase in the value of their house would be tremendous.

"Okay, let's look into it."

"Really?" Her voice rose.

He winked. "Yes, really. Perhaps it's time we look into some home improvements, or just search for something newer."

Her face lit up. "Okay. I'll ask around and get some referrals. Maybe we can meet with some folks later this week."

To bring her utter happiness, he'd buy her the Biltmore.

Later that week, Angie had everything unboxed and her office mostly put together. The move for her and Nicci had gone off without a hitch.

Angie grinned, looking down at the ladies' restroom sink as she washed her hands. Why was it that everything felt better when she and Mac were in tune? Why was it that everything felt better since she was having incredible sex with Mac?

She didn't know she could enjoy sex so much. This time around might be even hotter than when they'd first started dating—as if their familiarity allowed them to be more free and uninhibited. Not to mention, his stamina now was much better than his twenties.

But it was so much more than just sex. They were reconnecting.

Katy, l'Amour's VP of Operations and Logistics, exited a stall and met her gaze in the mirror. Katy was a few inches shorter than Angie, but the pants' suits she wore made her look taller. Angie had met her partner a few years back at a happy hour after work. Katy and Bri had the same sense of humor, the same quick wit, and the same love for each other. They were two halves of the same whole.

"You look happy. Is it because the fifth floor offices are finished and you're getting the best one?"

She flashed a smile to Katy as she dried her hands. "Hey, Katy. Yeah, something like that."

"Well, it looks good on you."

"Thanks. Listen, I've been meaning to ask you. You and Bri remodeled your house last year. Did you like the company you hired?"

She tipped her head slightly. "We did. Are y'all thinking about remodeling your house?"

"Yes. Well, that or moving into something bigger."

"Good for you. If you want, I'll dig out his name and email it you. I do know a realtor, too. He's been in the area for *years*. Really knows his way around."

"Yeah? That would great. Thanks."

"You're welcome."

Angie strode back to her office. What a serendipitous trip, she thought. Things were definitely flowing these days. *What a sharp contrast from a few weeks ago.*

CHAPTER
TWENTY-FIVE

Mac read from his tablet at the kitchen table and glanced at the time—a little over an hour before the boys would be dropped off from their practices.

The doorbell rang, and Angie went to answer it. That would be the real estate agent Angie had learned about from a woman in her office. What was his name? Bradley something.

He rather liked the contractor, Earl, they'd met two nights ago. They'd shared their ideas about the house. Earl had agreed, then added a few ideas of his own. They'd discussed bumping out a wall in the master bedroom, leaving room to expand the bathroom. In addition, they could take out a wall between the breakfast nook and family room, opening the whole area. The house needed more remodeling, but some things would have to wait. They would take the projects one at a time.

Angie had agreed with him to pay Earl the few hundred bucks needed to generate a computer design so they could see the full scope of the new layout—he was anxious to see what it would look like.

Mac had to admit, it felt good. Maybe because this was what Angie really wanted. Maybe because it represented a fresh start for both of them. Mac didn't care about the reason. Knowing he and Angie were moving forward and trying to fix their broken marriage meant everything to him. He felt it deep in his bones—they had something worth salvaging.

He heard some chattering at the front door, as Angie showed the agent into the house. The voice sounded rather feminine. Mac closed his tablet cover and stood as Angie and the agent entered the kitchen.

The floor dropped out from underneath him.

There, in front of him, stood Victoria. The woman he had almost fucked a few months before. The breath left his lungs, and his chest seized up like a rhino sat on him. Her eyes went wide, but Victoria recovered quickly.

"Victoria, this is my husband, Mac. Mac, this is Victoria Hemming."

Wearing a skirt suit, her hair pulled back, Mac wasn't fooled by the eyeglasses she wore. She held out her hand for a shake. Mac swallowed hard, and looking down, he took it. "Nice to meet you, Ms. Hemming." He forced a smile.

What the fuck was she doing in his house?

He turned toward Angie, keeping his expression as neutral as possible. "I thought you had Bradley coming to see us."

Angie tipped her head ever-so-slightly. "Victoria is from Bradley's office. He was on an appointment so Victoria's here instead." Angie faced the realtor and said, "Please, have a seat."

Victoria glided to the table as though she hadn't a care in the world, like a tornado that could wreck a town and move on to the next. From her high-gloss hair to her excessive makeup, she wasn't real. Her emotions weren't real.

She'd paid big bucks to have the kind of polish Angie had naturally. How in the hell did he ever think she was attractive? Sure, he'd been drunk, but still. Angie was real, with a heart of gold that anyone would envy. Victoria had *nothing* on Angie.

"Mr. and Mrs. MacKey, I can assure you, I am *very* experienced, and although I would be your listing agent, you get the power of the whole office working to sell your house."

Mac jumped on that. "Oh, of course, and I meant no offence. Angie and I are actually considering a few different options. Selling the house is one of them. So why don't you tell us about your services." *Do I need to tell you that I'm only asking about your* professional *services?*

The low bubble of anger in his gut sped to a full-on boil. This woman, sitting across from him in his house, had made a play for him. And now, she had the gall to come into his home, and try and convince him to let her sell it for them.

She had to know the owner's names before she accepted the appointment.

Victoria started with her spiel about knowing the area and having buyers ready to view whenever they were ready to put it on the market. She laid out her marketing plan and how the house would be priced. Mac was certain she'd given that speech thousands of times before.

But he would not give her the satisfaction of riling him up. He made sure he appeared calm and relaxed. He smiled occasionally, mostly to his wife. He had a second chance with Angie, and he would not let Victoria come in and fuck it up.

Angie rose and Victoria followed. "Let me show you around."

She needs to go. He blotted his brow. If she even thought of saying something to Angie, she would regret it for as long as he lived.

Angie took her on a brief tour, and they returned to the foyer. Mac stood waiting. The sooner Victoria got out, the better.

"Well, thank you so much. It was great meeting you both," the realtor said.

"You too," Angie replied.

"I'll touch base with you in a few days." She held out a hand.

"Sounds good. That will give me and Mac some time to think it over."

Mac opened the door for her. "Have a nice night, Ms. Hemming."

They said their goodbyes and Mac closed the door, maybe too harshly. There was no way in hell she was selling their home, if he and Angie decided to sell.

"What did you think?" he asked Angie as they strolled back into the kitchen.

"I like her. What do you think?"

Mac tipped his head. "Uh, I think we can do better. Her speech felt a little canned. Maybe we should get some other realtors to interview, if we decide to go that route."

Angie felt that something was off. There was nothing wrong with Victoria, but Angie sensed Mac didn't like the realtor the moment she'd walked in. He'd acted cool and terse toward her. That was not Mac's style. Even if he didn't like someone, he could hide it well enough.

Sirens went off in Angie's head, and loudly. She sent a silent prayer to the heavens that she was wrong.

"I sorta liked her." She bit the inside of her cheek. "But I definitely got the impression you didn't like her from the get-go."

"What?" He stacked the papers on the kitchen table and then filled his glass from the water pitcher.

"Have you met her before?"

Mac maintained eye contact, but blinked a few times. "I am merely making judgments on the job I think Victoria

248

would do for us," he said, not addressing her question. "I just think it would be wise to interview other realtors as well."

"That's the first time you called her Victoria."

Mac licked his lips. "What is it, Angie?"

She lifted her nose in the air. No sense dancing around her issue. "Mac, my gut is screaming at me right now, that you know this woman. If that's the case, why aren't owning up to it? Because that tells me you have something to hide. Please, tell me I'm wrong."

Mac looked down and ran a hand over his brow and through his hair. He raised his gaze back to her. He didn't say a word. And the longer the silence, the deeper her horror spread. She felt the tiny pricks at the back of her eyes.

What is he not saying?

He reached for her hand, and she let him. "Angie, it was while we were separated. I realized what a mistake I was about to make and ended it immediately. It meant nothing."

God no! She yanked her hand back and crossed her arms in front of her. "So, you not only know her...you almost had sex with that woman?" she said as she pointed toward the front door.

Blood roared in her ears. Her heart pounded in her chest so hard, she feared it might explode.

Again, he didn't say a word. Then he nodded. "Almost. I don't want her—"

"Shut up!" She stepped back.

This can't be happening, she thought.

Oh, God. "How could you do this?"

Mac's eyes showed dull and sorrowful. "It was a mistake. I was drunk and not thinking clearly. It's never happened before, and—"

"Stop it! Don't say it." The tears that threatened to spill, let loose, and streamed down her cheeks. "I can't trust anything that comes out of your mouth." She shook her head. She needed space.

She felt like they were in a movie, like this wasn't real. Another hour, the story would have a happen ending and the credits would roll. "How could this happen?" she said to no one. "I never cheated on you when we were separated." She pointed her finger at him, her face hot.

"Angie, please. Let me explain."

"No!" She sobbed. She braced one hand on the counter and covered her face with the other. She wanted to crawl out of her skin. Then she lowered her voice and said, "You need to leave." She looked him dead in the eyes. She was so hurt and angry, she could hardly see straight. To think she was allowing him back in. What a fool!

His gaze turned glassy. "Please, Angie. I'm sorry. I'm so sorry. I want to work this out."

"I don't see how we can. I need space. Go." With those parting words, she turned, walked into the bedroom and closed the door.

She stood against the door and waited. Finally, she

heard the garage door close, and she let herself sink to the ground.

She sobbed so loud, she didn't recognize her own voice. A kick in the stomach would've been less painful, a severed limb . . . the man had just ripped out her heart and laid it out on their tile floor for her to watch it shrivel and die. She covered her face with her hands. How could this happen? They were on the right track. They were getting back together. How could he? She'd trusted him. Goddammit!

He'd made a fool of her. She should have never let him move back in.

Not to mention, the boys were expected back soon, and she had no idea what to tell them. Damn him! Damn him!

Mac drove out of town with no clue as to where he was headed. Cold sweat trickled down his neck.

How had this happened? He'd won Angie back. He got his wife back.

He'd been listening to her, really listening. He complimented her more. He'd held her hand the few times they'd gone out. He paid attention to her, and he could see the difference. She was letting him back in. They were reconnecting, and bam! Happiness disappeared in an instant.

His greatest fear realized.

He'd fucked up being with Victoria, and fucked up

again not thinking he would ever run into her. He thought he'd hidden his reaction well enough when he saw the woman walk into his house. How in the world had Angie picked up on it?

His car pulled into an empty parking spot in front of a liquor store. He stepped out of the car and went inside in search of a liter of his favorite whiskey. His plan—drink himself into oblivion.

After some more driving, he found a hotel on the outskirts of Dallas—quiet and away from anyone he might fucking know.

He looked in the backseat and noticed his trusty gym bag. Clean clothes, shoes, and a few toiletries. He had to believe all he needed was one night's worth of clothes. He would call Angie the next day and hope like hell she wouldn't hang up on him. He could repair this. She just needed time. Time to absorb the blow, then realize it was before they had reconciled, and she was sure to forgive him when she calmed down.

How did this happen?

Sipping from the glass, he scanned the room. He'd stayed at a thousand hotels like this over the years. They all looked and felt the same—neutrals colors, nothing too offensive, and no Angie. He didn't want to be in some crappy hotel room. He wanted to be home. Home was Angie.

He glanced at his phone after his second drink, eager

for a text or voicemail from Angie. Even yelling at him, at least she'd be talking to him. Nothing.

He rubbed his eyes. He'd lost the woman he loved, all in a moment of weakness. Of course, he had only himself to blame.

Hell, you brought this on yourself.

She didn't care how much you made or how hard you worked. Angie just wanted you. Your time and attention. How hard was that to give?

He loved this woman. Had since the moment he'd laid eyes on her.

He took another sip and replayed the day over and over, like witnessing a wreck in slow-motion. His stomach roiled. He felt like shit. He flipped the channels some more, hoping to numb himself along with his fifth glass of whiskey. He hadn't cried in . . . years. This could be the night.

CHAPTER TWENTY-SIX

Monday morning Angie dragged her body into the office. Two days since she'd learned about Mac's cheating and threw him out. Unfortunately, makeup did little to hide the dark circles or add color to her pale skin.

"Good morn— Oh, hell. What happened to you?" Nicole's eyes rounded.

Angie looked down while she turned on her computer. She shook her head, but couldn't speak. She already felt tears gathering at the thought of explaining what had happened.

"C'mon. Bring your purse," Nicci said as she took Angie's hand and led her to the ladies' lounge.

They sat, Nicci still holding her hand. "Tell me what's going on."

Angie had to tell Nicci what had happened. She trusted her friend to the ends of the earth, and she needed to unload this heavy burden. She'd been half-tempted to call Nicci that weekend to confide in her.

She took in a deep breath and began. "We had a real

estate agent come by the house Saturday to talk to us about selling it. Katy gave me the name. Well, the agent she recommended couldn't come, so he sent someone else from his office. A woman," her voice croaked unexpectedly. "Mac, knew her. I could feel it, so I asked him about it and he did."

She blinked and several tears let loose before she could continue.

Nicci squeezed her hands.

"I had a sense that something was off, Nicci. I asked him if he'd slept with her. He said he had, once."

Nicci furrowed her brow. "What did you do?"

"I told him to leave. I haven't seen or talked to him since Saturday. Oh God, Nicci. What do I do?"

"Oh, sweetie. I don't know. Do you believe it was only the once?"

Angie thought about it. That question had crossed her mind endless times this past weekend. "My gut tells me yes, it's only been the one time."

"Was it while you two were separated?"

Angie nodded. "But that doesn't matter. He said he wanted—always wanted—to get back together with me. No one does that if they're trying to get back with their wife." She wiped her cheek briskly.

Her blood pressure climbed as anger covered the pain and despair. "What the hell?"

"I know. Don't make any rash decisions. You've been so happy these last few weeks—excited about remodeling or even selling." Nicci smoothed her thumbs over the backs of Angie's hands. "Excited that you two were reconciling and about Mac moving back in." She inhaled. "All I'm suggesting is that you give it some time, sweetie."

Angie's head dropped forward and tears fell on her skirt.

Nicole leaned forward and wiped Angie's cheeks with a tissue. "Can you give it a little time?"

Could she? Angie hadn't been able to sleep at all since Mac left. The boys were sullen and quiet *again* when she'd told them that she and their father had more work to do if they were to reconcile. She cried because she was sad, depressed, and embarrassed.

She nodded to Nicci, who wrapped her in a hug. "Of course you can. Give it a few days, then you two can sit down and talk."

"I suppose," she responded because really what was a few days or weeks? She certainly had no plans. No Fabio waiting in the wings to whisk her off to a tropical island. She sighed heavily.

After another minute, Angie fixed her makeup and walked back to her office, aware of being on the clock.

Jarmon buzzed her line a few hours later. He sounded panicked. Some designers were having trouble keeping up with demand. He asked her to meet with him, the buyers, and distribution.

In many respects, this was a good problem to have—

the market loved what l'Amour was selling. Their clientele was excited about the new men's line and were buying it up. Production couldn't keep pace with demand.

Angie reassured Jarmon she would send out a press release with the proper spin on it. In the meantime, the buyers needed to make sure production would be equipped to handle the full company-wide rollout next year. It was one thing to have issues during a test market, but that wouldn't be allowed once there was a full roll-out.

Angie was just grateful for the distraction. Anytime she thought about Mac, her heart ached. She replayed Saturday over and over, and each time her stomach knotted. He'd called several times and sent a few text messages. She couldn't bring herself to listen to the messages. She couldn't understand how he could cheat on her when they were on the road to recovery.

At five-fifteen, Nicci strolled into Angie's office.

"How did you do today?"

She looked up from her screen, not wanting to think about the day ending. That meant going home to upset boys, and she positively hated that they were going through all this shit.

"I survived."

"Anything I can do?"

"No, that's okay." Then she remembered Stuart's playoff game. "Wait. There is something. Care to come with me to Stuart's football game Friday? I don't know if I could handle the possibility of facing Mac alone."

Nicci's eyes softened. "Sure. I'll swing by and pick you up about seven?"

"Thanks. That'd be great."

"I'm heading out. You want me to wait for you?"

"No. I have another twenty minutes of work to finish."

"Okay. Take care, babe. I'll see you tomorrow." Nicci slung her coat over her arm and turned to leave.

Angie had managed to get through the day, and stay focused on work. The "after work", being at home, alone with her thoughts, would be her problem. How could she get through the next few days or weeks? And the holidays were right around the corner.

Her life had spun off its axis. She missed Mac, and so desperately wanted to take him back, but the pain at the thought of him being with another woman held her back. He'd betrayed her, them, and even if she could get past the pain, how to trust that it would never happen again? She didn't think it would, but hell, she'd been wrong about quite a lot lately. She didn't trust her instincts.

One day at a time. Hell, one hour at a time.

Mac found concentrating on work nearly impossible. Mimi scrutinized him the first morning he arrived late to work, and to her credit, deflected as much attention off of him as possible.

This time away from Angie was even worse than when he'd moved out months ago. He'd hurt her, and the look on her face would haunt him until the day he died.

He couldn't blame her. If she'd had sex with another guy, fury would have taken him over, the likes of which he'd probably never experienced before. But instead of pushing her away, he'd pull her close. He'd claim her. He'd want to change the image in her head of some asshole to him. She'd know who she belonged to. For hours, he'd caress her, kiss her from head to toe, make love to her in every imaginable way. Probably spank her. Another man would never enter into her mind again; she would cream at the thought of what *he* could do to her, for her. She would beg for more.

Now he was begging . . . for forgiveness.

He finished an email to his sales team, then yanked a sheet of paper from the printer. Time to write that love letter Ryan suggested.

My dearest Angie,

Words cannot express how sorry I am for what I put you through. Not just for the infidelity, but for years of neglect. You are my world, and I took you for granted. I know I may not deserve this, but I am begging for your forgiveness.

When we said our vows eighteen years ago, I told you I would cherish you until the day I die. I meant it, and I still do.

The truth is, I don't deserve someone as beautiful as you. You wanted me, not my money or my gifts. You patiently waited years for me to figure that out. I'm praying that now that I have, it isn't too late.

You are my life, and my soul. I am broken without you. If you take me back, I will spend every day proving that to you. It is what you deserve.

I love you with every fiber of my being.

He gave it once last glance, signed it, and picked up the phone to call the florist.

"No," he said to no one. "That won't cut it."

Mac knew he had one shot at getting her back. He opened the website of the Catholic cathedral where they were married. Bingo!

He buzzed his admin. "Mimi, do we have any photo paper?"

"Uh, yes. Bottom right cabinet in your bookcase. Want me to get it for you?"

"No. I got it. Thanks."

He found the box and set up the printer. After trimming the image, he scribbled across the back, loaded everything in an envelope, and addressed it to her work.

He walked out to Mimi's desk. "Would you please get a courier to deliver this? I'd do it myself, but as you know, I have a meeting in fifteen."

She gave him a sympathetic smile—probably well aware something big went down—and replied, "Absolutely. Right away."

"Thanks." He spun around to leave and crossed his fingers that the apology would at least open her up to talking. At least . . .

CHAPTER TWENTY-SEVEN

A ngie and Nicci descended the bleacher steps, heading to the parent section. Robbie took off for the student section. Angie knew Mac would be at the game, but that didn't mean she had to sit near him. They were both on the home side cheering on the Fighting Knights to a win, and hopefully moving on to the next playoff game and one step closer to state champions.

Angie saw Mac almost immediately a few sections over in front of the fifty-yard line. A few days earlier, she'd received his letter at work. The note and the photo were so beautiful, so touching, she'd bawled like a baby. She'd ran to the bathroom for privacy, and knew she had to do something. She didn't know what exactly, and the indecisiveness was ruining her.

Angie felt no better at the game. The weight in her stomach felt like bricks. She was uncomfortable with the whole situation, but that didn't matter. Supporting Stuart and the team was paramount. Just a few hours, she told herself, and she could go home.

Stuart had been put in for several plays during the last few games, and that boded well for his chances to play in this game.

Occasionally, Angie'd peer over in Mac's direction. He looked like hell—bags under his eyes, shoulders slumped, barely any enthusiasm when the Knights scored. How had it gotten so bad so fast?

Catching her looking his way, Nicci asked, "How are you doing?"

Angie sighed. "I'm okay."

"Do you want to go over at halftime and say something to Mac?"

"No," she answered quickly. "That's the *last* thing I want to do. I don't want to risk losing it with all these people around."

"Okay." Nicci reached over, grabbed her hand, and gave it a squeeze.

The game continued and Stuart went in for three plays. Halftime featured both school's bands, cheerleaders, and color guard, and she noticed Mac made himself scarce.

After halftime, the Fighting Knights received the ball and ran all the way to their forty-five yard line. The score was fourteen-seventeen with the Knights leading.

"Oh, Stuart's back in." Nicci pointed with her chin.

Anxious, but excited for him, Angie focused on her son. He played wide receiver, so she suspected it might be a passing play.

The whistle blew, and the center hiked the ball. The quarterback dropped back, Stuart ran, but in no time the defense broke through the offensive line and sacked the quarterback. The home crowd moaned.

The second-down play Stuart ran long and then cut in toward the center of the field as the quarterback searched for an open receiver. Stuart was open. The quarterback threw the ball in Stuart's direction.

"Oh, Nicci," Angie muttered in tamed excitement. They all watched the perfect spiral sail through the air.

"It's a little high," Nicci said what everyone saw.

Stuart timed his jump and gave all he had to reach up and grab the ball out of the air. The crowd rose to its feet as he hugged the ball into his body. Angie held her breath when she saw two defenders coming from both sides, heading right for Stuart. He didn't see them. Everything moved as if in slow motion. The defenders both collided with him at the same time, and the impact could be heard in the bleachers. One of the defender's helmets hit Stuart's.

Angie gasped and watched as Stuart fell to the ground like a ragdoll. "Oh no." Her hands flew over her gaping mouth. She turned to the right and met Mac's eyes. His face was taut and his eyes rounded.

The coaches ran onto the field and huddled down around Stuart. She couldn't see what was going on, but too much time had passed—Stuart had been knocked out. Both teams bent down on a knee. More men ran onto the field.

"Oh God, Nicci." Tears welled in her eyes. "Tell me he'll be alright."

Several more moments passed with no sign of movement from Stuart. When Angie heard the ambulance's siren in the distance, she jumped up and nearly ran down the bleachers. Mac had already made it to her end of the stands and waited for her at the bottom.

"Let's get on the field," he said in a tight, anxious voice.

Mac knew where to enter the field and no one denied them access. His hand guided her as they hustled to see their son.

"Mac, Mrs. MacKey," the coach said. "Stuart's been knocked unconscious. Medics are coming—" As if on cue, paramedics raced on the field carrying a stretcher.

She peered down at her son through the coaches gathered around. The color was gone from his face. Angie covered her mouth with her hand. The whole thing felt surreal. The crowd fell silent, and all eyes were on the scene on the field. Every parent in the audience knew exactly what Angie and Mac were going through right then.

This cannot be happening.

Mac felt helpless, standing there, watching his son out cold, and not knowing when he'd wake up. The medics worked to carefully secure Stuart on the stretcher.

He glanced at Angie. She wiped tears that had streamed down her cheeks. Her somber face pale, and worry lines etched into her forehead.

"He's going to be alright," he told her, hoping to give her optimism, praying the words were true. Stuart *had* to be alright.

The coach approached them again. "Do you want to go in the ambulance with him?"

"Yes," Angie replied as she started to follow the people carrying her son.

Suddenly, she stopped and turned to face him. "Robbie?"

He put his hand on her shoulder to point her to the right. "He's right here."

Robbie carried the same worry lines as his mother. "Matt said I can stay with him, Mom. I'll be fine. Go be with Stuart."

Tears formed in her eyes again, as she reached for her youngest and pulled him in for a hug. Shortly, she backed away and kissed his forehead.

"I'll take my car and meet you at the hospital," Mac told her.

She nodded and turned to Nicci.

"Go to the hospital. I'll be fine. Call me later." Nicci rubbed her back.

Mac and Robbie walked off the field, feeling the weight of the world on them. Mac thanked Matt's mom for taking Robbie.

"I'll call you later," he told his son.

"Okay, Dad."

Mac jogged through the parking lot to his car and took off as fast as he comfortably could.

God, please help Stuart. Please help him to be okay.

He had to keep it together. Stuart would be okay. He *had* to be okay. Mac's world had crashed all around him, but he could at least count on his boys being safe and healthy. Stuart *had* to wake up.

He raced to the hospital, probably breaking a dozen laws, but he didn't have time to worry about that. He ran into the ER and saw Angie talking with a nurse.

"He just woke up," the nurse reported, "but he has trouble answering questions and following directions. They are taking him for a CT scan. Please have a seat, folks, and the doctor will be out shortly."

Angie let out a little breath, rubbing her hands over her arms.

"He's awake. That's progress," Mac said, wanting so much to believe. Willing it to be true.

"Yes, I suppose you're right," she replied meekly.

"C'mon, let's sit. Do you want anything?"

She shook her head. "Just for him to be okay."

Mac understood that.

After several moments in silence, Angie whispered, "I don't think I've ever felt so helpless, Mac."

He reached for her hand and held it. There was nothing he could say. They both felt the same way. Anxious, worried, like life as they knew it was hanging by a thread.

They filled out a ton of paperwork, and waited. Hours passed before the doctor finally came to see them. They quickly stood. "How is he?"

"Your son is awake. You can see him. I'd like to keep him overnight. He's had some vomiting and a headache, which is all to be expected with a concussion of this severity. I expect him to make a full recovery though."

Mac squeezed his wife's hand and glanced her way to see the first sign of hope in her eyes.

They followed the doctor, and saw Stuart lying on the bed, monitors and tubes surrounding him.

"Mom. Dad." His voice sounded groggy.

"Stuart." Angie leaned over to hug and kiss him. "How are you?"

Mac did the same, careful not to snag any tubes connected to his son. His face was still pale, but color was slowly returning.

"Guys, I'll be fine," Stuart said as he noticed the tears streaming down Angie's cheeks. "I just want to know if we won the game. Do you know?"

Mac had to smile. A sure sign his son would be alright.

"Stuart, perhaps you should focus on getting better," Angie said with a small smile on her lips.

They chatted a bit more, and the doctor came in, reminding them that the hospital would be monitoring him overnight.

"Will you please call us if there is any change in Stuart's condition?" Mac asked.

The doctor said he would and encouraged them to go home.

Mac glanced back at their son, and saw his eyelids half-closed. Stuart needed rest.

"We'll be back in the morning, Stuart. Get some sleep." Mac leaned over and kissed his son's forehead.

Angie whispered something in Stuart's ear, then kissed his cheek.

They walked out as the doctor gave final instructions to the nurse on duty.

Suddenly, Mac felt ten years older. And tired. So incredibly tired.

His life had spiraled out of control, and he knew he had only himself to blame. He'd taken Angie for granted. He'd taken them all for granted.

"Nicci drove us to the stadium. Would you please drive me home?" Angie's voice snapped him out of his wallowing.

"Of course."

They rode in silence. Other than giving her another apology, there was nothing to say. This was not the time to have that conversation.

He pulled into the driveway and walked her inside, flipping on several lights, and making sure the house was secure. He shot Robbie a text to tell him Stuart would be okay. Mac didn't like the idea of leaving Angie alone that night, but it wasn't his choice.

He missed his wife with an ache, but he knew why she'd thrown him out. He scolded himself inside, repeatedly.

Angie pulled out a kitchen chair and slumped down into it. She set her purse on another chair and starting removing her shoes.

"Everything looks okay." He stood several feet away.

She looked up at him, dark circles under her eyes.

"I'll leave and lock up behind me. I can pick you up in the morning, and we can go to the hospital together."

She nodded. "Okay."

He wanted to say more, so much more. But instead he just turned and walked toward the front door. To a fucking lonely hotel room.

He'd barely clasped the door knob, when he heard Angie's sob coming from the kitchen.

CHAPTER TWENTY-EIGHT

Mac spun around and high-tailed it to Angie. His eyebrows pulled together. *Shit!* She'd collapsed to her shins on the kitchen floor, her hands over her face, sobbing heavily.

He went down to the floor in front of her and wrapped his hands around her forearms. "Angie?"

When she raised her head, he was hit by the tears streaming from her eyes—his strong wife, so wounded.

He lifted her to her knees and pulled her close. He didn't care if she was mad or not. She needed comfort. He understood that. He wrapped his arms around her, and she cried harder.

Tears began to collect in his eyes too.

"He'll be okay, Ang." He stroked a hand over her back. "Shh."

"I know." A sob escaped. "What happened, Mac?"

Her question hit him head-on. She wasn't crying for Stuart. She was crying for them.

What could he say?

"I feel like I let you down, the boys down. Myself down." She covered her face again.

"No." He kissed her forehead. "You are amazing. I screwed it up. I'm so sorry for everything I did to hurt us. Shh." He kissed her damp cheek.

She sobbed.

"I'm so sorry I took you for granted," he said softly at her ear. A tear ran down his face.

"I miss you," she said in between cries. Then her arms swung around his neck.

He held her tighter. God, his heart was breaking. "Shh." He kissed her cheek, her neck, like he could kiss away her hurt. Their hurt.

"I miss you so much. I am so sorry. I was stupid. All I can hope is that you forgive me. Someday." He'd hold her for as long as she'd let him.

Her sobs slowed and her breathing began to level out. He hated himself for causing her this pain.

"Don't leave. Please stay with me. I can't be alone tonight."

He didn't want to be alone either. This might be the last time he could spend a night with his wife, beside his wife.

"Okay." He stood upright and helped her rise. She walked to the bedroom and he followed.

He stripped down to his undershirt and briefs, as he often slept in the winter, and slid into bed.

Angie exited the bathroom in a bathrobe. She flipped off the bedside lamp, the only illumination coming from the street light outside.

She slipped off her robe and climbed into bed beside him.

They both laid in the darkness, a heavy silence lingering in the air. Mac stared at the nothingness, rewinding the events that brought him to this point.

After several long moments, she spoke. "I was so scared for Stuart. I just watched and watched, and he didn't move."

He stretched his arm, found her hand and cupped it in his. "Me too. But he'll be okay."

"Thank God."

She rolled to her side and asked softly, "Please hold me, Mac."

He shuffled closer and reached for her. She snaked her arms around his neck and nuzzled close to him. Mac contained his surprise when he pulled her close and found her naked. Wrapping his arms around her torso, her warm, soft skin felt amazing to his touch. He was afraid he would get hard holding her, and she would throw him out of bed. Sweat beads broke out on his forehead as he tried to contain his lust at holding his beautiful wife again. Her body flush against his felt marvelous. It always had, he'd just forgotten that too many times.

"I'm tired of being sad," she spoke quietly at his ear.

"I know, and I'm to blame for that."

"No," she pulled back to look at him.

He could barely make out her facial features in the dim light.

"I'm to blame too." She pressed her lips to his. "I'm to blame too."

"I miss you, Angie. My heart aches every day for you."

"Mac," she breathed.

Her body pressed closer to him, and she kissed him again. This time his lips parted slightly and her tongue stroked them. A groan slipped out when she dove into his mouth wholly.

She wanted him and he wanted her, and they could have this night. This night they could be there for each other, comfort each other.

One arm slid off his shoulder to the hem of his T-shirt and she pushed it upward, exposing his abdomen. He didn't fight his growing erection anymore.

He lifted off the bed so she could push the T-shirt off entirely. He laid over her, gently pushing her into the mattress. His cock nestled between her legs, and he covered her lips with his.

Her legs swung around his hips, her heels resting on the back of his thighs. He angled his head to take the kiss deeper. He needed to be deep inside her, to connect with her. Be one again.

He broke the kiss only long enough to speak his heart.

"I love you, Angie. I've always loved you."

"Mac, please make love to me."

And he would. He would savor every precious moment with her.

He pushed back and roamed her body with his mouth. Her neck, her delicious breasts, her smooth stomach. Bending her legs, he pushed them wider apart. He caressed her slick sex with the tip of his finger and listened as she gasped. Stroking her warm, swollen pussy, he heard her breathing increase. He slowly pushed one finger into her core. Then he leaned down and slid his tongue over her burgeoning clit. Her aroma filled his nostrils and he hungered to be inside her. His cock ached.

He caressed her for several more moments, feeling her slickness grow, before he rose off the bed and stood.

"Mac?"

"Just a moment, baby." He shed his briefs, getting himself ready for her.

He returned to the bed to find her just as he'd left her—spread open, waiting for him.

"You're beautiful, Angie. I'll want you for the rest of my life." He positioned himself over her, and with his hands, he leveraged her hips higher as he slowly pushed inside her insanely soft heat.

"Oh," she breathed as she reached for his face, bringing him to her.

"Let me." He pumped slowly, rhythmically. The angle

would hit her sweet spot just right. "Let me make love to you for the rest of your life."

She moaned into his mouth, gripping his hair between her fingers.

"Let me love you."

"Mac. Oh God, don't stop. Please, baby."

His pumping gained speed. "Let me show you how much you mean to me."

She gasped for air now. He felt her inner muscles twitch. She was close.

"I love you, Angie."

"Ah. I love you, Mac." Her breath was as ragged as his. "Always."

Her muscles clenched tight around his cock. She cradled him in the best possible way. Her arms, her pussy, her heart. In a short span of time, he'd almost lost the woman that meant the most to him. He would never let that happen again.

"Come, baby."

She cried out his name in her orgasm, and it was like a wave of euphoria over him. He pumped harder now.

"I'm never letting you go, Angie." He pulled out his hands, grabbed her face, and dove into her mouth. And he drove deeper into her.

His balls drew up, and he released all he had—all the tension, pain, lust—and felt renewed in her arms again.

He collapsed, leaning on one elbow to protect her.

Their accelerated breathing was the only sound in the room.

He slowly slid out of her, lying to her side, and drew her close into him.

After a brief moment, she kissed his chest and lifted her head. "I forgive you. I don't want to be without you. My heart aches without you, too."

Her words were like a panacea to his heart and his soul. He took in air, a clear breath he didn't think he'd ever have again.

"I love you, Angie. I'm miserable without you. My life is full with you in it."

"Mac, I need you, and I don't want to be without you again," she whispered before she kissed him softly. She sighed as she tucked her head into his chest.

He swept his hands across her back. "Sleep, baby." He pecked the top of her head.

They both needed sleep. Tomorrow was a new day, a day to start rebuilding their future. Stuart was going to be alright. And Mac miraculously had his wife back. He wouldn't lose her again.

Angie awoke to the smell of coffee. She opened her eyes to the sight of the cup on the nightstand and Mac sitting on the side of the bed, looking down at her. From the looks of it, he'd dug out some blue jeans and a fresh shirt from the closet.

"How long have you been watching me?"

"Hours," he said with a straight face.

"Liar."

"I couldn't help myself. You looked so peaceful." His eyes had a gentleness and sincerity to them. A look she hadn't seen often, one she missed.

"Did the hospital call?"

"No, I called them though. Stuart is doing fine. When he finishes breakfast, they want to run a few tests. Depending on the results, he could come home today."

"That's good news." She sat, the sheet loosely wrapping her naked body, and reached for the coffee. "Mmm. Hits the spot. Thank you."

"You're welcome." There was a pause as he inhaled, as if he contemplated his next words. "Ang, we had an emotional few months, and definitely an emotional night. How are you?"

She stared down at her coffee, already having asked herself that same question. She'd slept better than she had in a *long* time, and was resolute in forgiving Mac. Sleeping with that woman—or whatever—was a stupid slip, and she knew deep inside she could trust him implicitly. There was this undefinable lightness in her heart, like she could breathe again. "First, I'll feel better when Stuart is home with us. But Mac, I meant it when I said I forgive you." She held his gaze. "I forgive all of it."

He blinked.

"I don't want to hang on to this resentment. Frankly,

I'd rather forget these last few months, if that's alright with you."

His mouth gaped. "You're serious?"

"Absolutely."

He paused a beat before he said, "I can't tell you how much I appreciate that. I don't want to forget these months. These months made me realize how desperately I need to be with you. How neglectful I'd become. That night in the hotel room with you, I never want to forget. You woke me up." He dropped to his knees before her and set her cup on the nightstand, taking her hands. "I don't deserve you," he whispered. "I hope we never need it, but the next time you say you want to see a counselor, I'll drop everything and go." He cradled the side of her face and gave her a little peck on her cheek, then her lips. "I'll fight for you."

Moisture gathered in her eyes.

He kissed her neck and her chest above the sheet. "How would you feel if we not forget *everything* about these last few months?" He gently pulled the sheet down, revealing her breasts. Warm kisses traveled the newly exposed skin.

She exhaled and closed her eyes, reveling in slow, warm trail of kisses. Her breathing turned shallow. "Yes, that sounds agreeable," she muttered.

"Then, lay back, Angelique."

Her eyes flew open. "Do we have time for this?"

He leaned forward kissing her mouth. "We have time,"

his tone firm. "Think of it as a massage, to warm you up, then we move this to the shower." With a hand at the nape of her neck, he lowered her to the mattress. He caressed her arms, sliding them over her head, while kissing and nipping at her throat.

She pushed her head into the mattress, arching for him. Her sex grew wet; she was putty in his hands.

He skimmed down her arms to her breasts, his thumbs toying with her nipples. Reaching a hand between them, he yanked the sheet off her body. "You're beautiful, Angie."

He dipped his tongue in her navel and moved south. Her hands reached for his hair.

"Over your head, baby. Remember, like a massage. Just lie there."

Oh, she wanted more. She writhed through his caresses up and down her thighs, his kisses avoiding the one place she was desperate to have him.

Finally, his tongue slid through her core, and she bowed off the bed. "Mmm," she moaned.

He made love to her with his mouth—warm and soft, easy but firm. Her slow climb toward orgasm had her panting. Her face grew hot. She was so close . . .

Suddenly, he stood, and claimed her in a heated tongue kiss. She could taste herself on him. "Shower."

She urgently wanted to come, but she now knew Mac wouldn't leave her hanging.

He blasted the water on high, and stripped off his shirt

while she worked on the jeans.

She quickly wrapped her hands on his hard, delicious cock. "Beautiful."

He grinned and tugged at her hand to follow him under the spray. He didn't say a word, merely placed her hands on the wall and pushed her legs apart with his knee. Water drenched their bodies. His hands slid up and down her back, over her ass, and to the inside of her thighs. "I could wake up every day like this, Angelique. Just having you squeeze my cock as you come, would make me feel like a king."

She moaned, letting her head fall back against his shoulder, while he gently separated her and pushed deep inside.

He groaned loudly, slipping right in. His movements gained speed as his hand reached around to stimulate her clit.

"Oh God." This wouldn't take long. Her hands plastered to the tile, as if she needed stability before collapsing.

Mac's thrusts and his circles over her clit were the perfect combination to put her over the edge. The orgasm shot from her center to every cell of her body. She called out his name just as he released inside of her.

His hands rested over hers as he panted at her neck. "Absolutely perfect."

"Mmm." He was right, it was perfect. If she could let

go, he would give her everything a woman needed from a man. Easier said than done sometimes, but she would work at it.

He pulled out and stroked her wet back. "Let's clean up and go to the hospital."

"Okay."

They got ready in amicable silence, fresh clothes and a fresh perspective. What a difference a day made.

She grabbed two yogurt drinks from the fridge and filled a travel cup with coffee.

With car keys in his hand, he asked, "Ready?"

She paused and set her purse on the counter. "Almost." She unzipped the interior pocket, retrieved her wedding ring, and slipped it on her finger.

He looked at her, unspoken gratitude in his handsome features.

"Ready now. Let's go get our son."

THE END.

If you enjoyed this story, please consider posting a review at one or more of your favorite retailers. Even a short review, one or two lines, can be a tremendous encouragement to the author. Your review is also a gift to other readers who may be searching for just this sort of story and will be grateful that you helped them find it.

Thank you!

OTHER BOOKS
BY MIA LONDON

Life To The Max
Wanton Angel, Prequel to Life To The Max

Perfect Seduction (Perfect, 1)
Perfect Surrender (Perfect, 2)

Beyond Lace (Hard Men of the Rockies, 4)

Undeniable Fate (Undeniable, 1)
Undeniable Love (Undeniable, 2)

Dry Spell (Sweet Escape, 1)
Hot Spell (Sweet Escape, 2)
Cold Spell (Sweet Escape, 3)

ABOUT THE AUTHOR

Mia London loves to write.

After reading fiction for years, she decided it was finally time to put those images and scenes floating around in her head down on paper.

She is a huge fan of romance, highly optimistic, and wildly faithful to the HEA (happily ever after). Her goal is to create a fantasy you will enjoy with characters you could love.

She lives in Texas with her attentive, loving, super-model husband, and perfectly behaved, brilliant children. Her produce never wilts, there are no weeds in her flowerbeds and chocolate is her favorite food group.

Facebook

Twitter

Instagram

Goodreads

www.mialondon.com

Email: mia@mialondon.com